DREAMS OF BETRAYAL
Realm of Nightmares

Steve R. Romano

WITH ILLUSTRATIONS BY:
STEVE R. & HEIDI BOSCH ROMANO

2021 Lunamont Visions Books Edition
Copyright © 2017 by Steve R. Romano

This story was written as a work of fiction. The names, characters, places and incidents are fictitious. Any resemblance to actual persons living or deceased, or to any business establishments, events, or locales, is entirely coincidental.

Lunamont Visions Books
Porterfield, Wisconsin 54159
LunamontVisionsBooks.com
books@Lunamont.com

Printed in the United States

Paperback: ISBN-13: 978-0-578-86550-8
eBook: ISBN-13: 978-0-578-86551-5

Publisher's Cataloging-in-Publication Data

Romano, Steve R.
Dreams of Betrayal: Realm of Nightmares / Steve R. Romano

p. cm.

ISBN-13: 978-0-578-86550-8
ISBN-10: 0-578-86550-5

1. FICTION / Science Fiction / Apocalyptic & Post-Apocalyptic
2. FICTION / Science Fiction / Action & Adventure
3. FICTION / Action & Adventure

Books by Steve R. Romano

Science Fiction

The Puppet Contingency
Dreams of Betrayal: The Vortex (Book 1)
Dreams of Betrayal: Realm of Nightmares (Book 2)
Dreams of Betrayal: Satellite of Doom (Book 3)
Dreams of Betrayal: Battle for Capernaum (Book 4)

Juvenile Fiction: Middle Grade

Mike and Scrag
Mike and Scrag: The Avalanche
Mike and Scrag: Thunder Ridge
Tony and the Haunted Goldmine

Children's Picture Books:

The Adventures of Amerina: The Garden
The Adventures of Amerina: The Doll
The Adventures of Amerina: The Horse
The Adventures of Amerina: The Sled

Author's website: SteveRRomano.com

ILLUSTRATIONS

ACKNOWLEDGMENTS

To my fans: thank you for your constant encouragement.

A special thanks to Heidi for her fine artwork, copy editing job and constant inspiration.

Prologue

Moleinar sat uncomfortably on a rickety wooden chair, the seat of which had been worn smooth by countless years of use. A worm-riddled pine table separated him from his reason for being in this dingy place at this unholy hour of the day—Apaula.

Moleinar watched with disgust as something wriggled through her filthy, matted brown hair. He didn't want to look, but he was morbidly compelled to stare in fascination at the multi-legged inhabitant as it went about its seemingly meaningful tasks. He idly wondered if it was searching for its morning meal and speculated as to just what it might feed on. Moleinar immediately regretted that line of thought and the accompanying mental image that formed in his mind. He felt his stomach lurch, followed by the sour taste of belly acid in his mouth. Choking back the throat-burning bile, he forced himself to look away before his breakfast of boiled pig fat made an unwanted resurgence.

His eyes roamed about the dimly lit room as if he searched for something, but in truth it sorely taxed his limited attention as he listened to her drone on about her "plan."

A single flickering lantern hung from a wrought iron hook behind the bar stand. The globe was so stained that only a faint amber glow escaped from within. It exuded the faint smell of flax oil, which did nothing to relieve the sour smell of vomit and alcohol that permeated the sawdust-covered floor.

The wooden spit buckets near each table saw little usage by the drunken patrons, who occasionally emptied their stomachs without aiming. Certainly, it was by no accident that this place was named the "Hawk 'n Spit."

The hour was early by the pub's weak standards, and as yet there were no other patrons besides himself and Apaula in the establishment. The absence of boisterous drunkards only made the drab, windowless place all that much more depressing.

His eyes drifted over towards the only other person in the bar—Sifty the barkeep.

Sifty was a rather short man who always seemed relaxed as he stood casually behind his counter, absently wiping out a never-ending line of glasses with a wet rag—the clean glasses he habitually placed upon a shelf built into the wall behind him.

To all outward appearances, he seemed completely unaware of the goings on in his bar; however, the truth was just the opposite. There was nothing he missed in even the minutest detail as he scrutinized his nightly clientele. He had diffused many a potential brawl over the years thanks to his vigilance, that and the hefty club he kept under the bar top.

Moleinar forced his attention back to Apaula while studiously avoiding any direct eye contact with her. He could not help but notice that nothing was astir in her wild village of hair. Evidently her multi-legged companion had sought a more fertile location. He felt a slight wave of revulsion move through his bowels.

Apaula Furter cleared her throat to show her irritation with Moleinar's inattention. She was the self-appointed matriarch of her little group of conspirators, of which Moleinar was one. She led the small cabal with the force of her will even though she lacked any real leadership skills, except of course her ability to push her weight around both literally and figuratively.

Hers was a coarse personality which seemed to endear only one other to her, and that was her very like-minded daughter. Her husband, Frank Furter, and their two sons had about as much backbone as a slug between the three of them, which suited Apaula's dominating personality just fine.

Moleinar tried to keep his thoughts far from this place as he involuntarily watched her probe her left nostril up to the second knuckle of her pudgy index finger. He suspected that should she go any deeper, she might retrieve some brain matter if any at all existed behind her unwashed forehead.

Her foraging digit wiggled and squiggled within her nostril, giving the impression of some living thing squirming its way deeper and deeper within the hair-lined passage. She forced her soot blackened finger another fraction of an inch. The thrust caused her left eye to turn inward and bug outward slightly. Her iris dilated and lost focus as she sought an elusive nugget of sticky mucus buried deep in her sinus cavity.

It was moments like these that gave Moleinar pause and had him on more than one occasion silently questioning his subservience to her. He was the captain of the guards, which deserved some respect. Maybe he should be the one to take over the land, a thought not too farfetched since he already commanded the township's drunken dragoons. He silently vowed to give the idea more consideration when he was somewhere else. He returned his focus to Apaula just in time to wish that he hadn't.

Her eyes uncrossed as she happily removed her trophy and sat back with a sigh of contentment, having successfully retrieved a gelatinous glob of snot that now dangled slippery wet from her fingertip. She briefly admired her handiwork in the dull red-orange coloring of the lamplight. The fiery hues danced within the mucus' milky depths in jewel like splendor. Apaula gazed admiringly into the viscous fluid, then she casually wiped the bodily goop on the underside of the table along with all the others. "What progress have you made?" she said calmly. But the look in her eyes conveyed a different message.

"We haven't yet found the opportunity to do away with the sentor." He tried to keep the disgust out of his voice, but to his ears it seemed that he'd failed miserably.

"What about the other one I asked you to find—this Laktos?"

"The sentor is sending me out with a detachment of guards later today to continue the search."

"Need I remind you of the importance of your part in all this?" she raised her voice in anger.

"No," he replied contritely.

"Good. In order for our planned overthrow of the sentor to succeed, we must give these drunken dragoons and the townsfolk a reason to want us as their new leaders."

"I have already swayed most of the current militia. They will follow us as long as we pay them in gold."

"That's good news," Apaula said. She raised one massive butt cheek off of her seat to more easily accommodate an explosion of flatulence before she continued. "But even the guards won't be enough to control the entire town should the people rebel against us. We must encourage them to follow us willingly."

"How will we do that?" Moleinar asked. He coughed slightly as a wave of noxious fumes wafted over and lingered. He tried to breathe without inhaling the intestine tainted smell of rotten eggs. The sour aftertaste in his mouth was a good indicator of his failure.

"By giving them something greater to fear. That's why we need this Laktos person. The rumors that persist about him since his arrival here last year will help us in our rebellion against the sentor."

"You're talking about the rumor of his being our deceased presider returned from the dead to seek his seat and unleash his retribution on the unholy? Am I right?"

"Yes," she replied dryly. "We can use this belief and expand on it." An idea was rapidly forming in her mind. "Imagine how terrified the people would become if they should find out that their fears about Laktos were true. And worse, that he was now here to seek his revenge on the town and its people for his demise."

Moleinar didn't get it, and worse, he made the mistake of letting his ignorance be known. "How will we convince Laktos to attack the village?"

"Idiot!" Apaula choked out the word in utter disbelief. How could anyone be as stupid as this man? "It does not matter whether or not Laktos attacks the town! All that's necessary is for the townspeople to believe that it's possible. When they fear it enough, they will gladly follow the first person to offer them protection from their demons. "I will—" She paused, then graciously added, "We will be those people. Laktos will be our unwitting and unknowing accomplice."

"If he is to be ignorant of our plans, then why do we need to find him?" Moleinar asked unwittingly.

"So he can't interfere later on. Imagine if he should actually turn up here and deny everything that we say about him. Do you think it would take long for the people to see he wasn't a threat?! What do you suppose they might do to us if they should find out that we betrayed their trust?"

"I hadn't thought of that," Moleinar said with just a hint of unease.

"Look. The entire town knows that Sentor Phu-Bar is searching for Laktos and his companions. Right?" Apaula inquired as if speaking to a moron.

"Yes."

"If you were to kill Phu-Bar, and we then blamed it on Laktos, nobody would suspect a thing. We could even say that the reborn presider's retribution had already begun with the slaying of Phu-Bar, thus creating a sense of urgency around the situation."

"I think I'm beginning to understand your point."

"All would agree that Phu-Bar is a powerful sentor. Consequently, with the sentor's death, it will be obvious that Laktos is a far greater threat. It will be relatively easy to convince the townsfolk of the horrific new enemy that lurks just over the horizon. The people's collective fear will fester and grow by the hour with each new rumor that spreads outwards from us to everyone listening. Laktos' armies will be approaching the township, even if only in fantasy. It won't be long until all the people of the land will beg us for protection from the approaching doom." A glint of obsession and greed sparkled in Apaula's eyes as she envisioned the scope of her deception.

Moleinar marveled at the simple logic of her reasoning. For an instant, he almost forgot the burning in his eyes.

Apaula continued her discourse engulfed in a sulfurous gas of her own making. "Laktos' armies will be the trumpet call of death." She emphasized her point with a pungent bugle blast of her own. "It doesn't matter that Laktos has no army, nor is even aware of any rebellion within the village. The single and most important thing is that the people of the town believe it—fear it body and soul."

"Yes," Moleinar whispered with a faraway look in his bloodshot eyes. "Then the way would be opened for us to rule the village," he mumbled. But secretly he desired to rule as the new magistrate and perhaps one day soon he would become the new sentor. But first their small clique had to eliminate Phu-Bar. And that was not going well, not well at all.

Later That Same Day

Captain Moleinar crept as silently as he could through snow nearly two-feet deep. The going was extremely arduous, with each footfall sinking down over his calf. Snow had long since packed his boots and he absently took notice that his feet had actually stopped hurting from the freezing cold—at least now that the numbness had become complete, he thought grimly. Odd how his thigh muscles could burn with the effort of just trying to walk, and yet his feet felt like two weighted stumps at the ends of his ankles as he plodded along.

He traversed across a slope of moderate incline, passing through a grove of hoarfrost blanketed trees. Their frozen branches closed in the surrounding area with an icy silence that seemed to stifle any sound. Even his very breath froze upon the frigid air as if in wait for some inexplicable thing to happen.

Spread out behind him followed fifteen of the village's diminishing militia. He wished that he commanded more. In fact, there'd been nearly seven times as many under his command a few scant weeks earlier. Unfortunately, Phu-Bar had suffered a serious defeat at the hands of an enemy who only he had survived. The loss of about a dozen men, including that serpent of a human Baub, was still an unexplained mystery to all but Phu-Bar. And it seemed unlikely that Phu-Bar would be talking about it any time soon.

Moleinar harbored no illusions that he might have survived on that mission. He certainly held no guilt for having been busy elsewhere when the others had been chosen to go. He had known most of the men who had died, had fought beside them many times. Whatever forces they had encountered must have been unbelievably powerful and deadly.

He certainly recognized the act of cowardice that had allowed the sentor to escape the same fate as his men. Moleinar knew that he would, without hesitation, sacrifice his men in order to save himself, just as it seemed the sentor had done.

With the sentor on his mind, Moleinar thought back on all the changes that had befallen the township since Phu-Bar's return. No, he realized that the troubles had started a few days prior to that over his own confrontation with that pub-crawler Sal Monella and his friend. His testicles twinged in sympathetic pain at the memory of his first encounter with Laktos. He really hated that man. Laktos was the reason for his being out in the cold, freezing his butt off. Phu-Bar wants him, Apaula wants him—hell, he wanted to find him so badly it hurt.

Moleinar would do just about anything to be rid of Laktos permanently, so he would stop hearing about him everywhere he went. It was because of Laktos, the sentor had ordered the town gates locked at sunset each night. Because of him anyone caught outside the fortress at night was subject to cruel punishment and faced immediate execution unless a substantial portion of their valuables made its way into the hands of Phu-Bar. It was because of Laktos, he could not satisfy his wife's lustful desires for the past week. Moleinar swore Laktos would suffer for his swollen genitals if nothing else.

A sharp creak echoed through the woods. He stopped short. Moleinar raised his right hand to signal a halt to the column of men. With a quick chopping motion, he sent them into hiding among the trees.

He could hear voices coming from somewhere further on. Moleinar cautiously moved forward, concentrating on the overheard words, but he could not yet understand them.

As he quietly crept closer to the unsuspecting people, he could make out individual conversations. He stooped lower and crept through a thicket of snow-covered brush. As he parted the shrubbery, he caught sight of a small band of people moving at a snail's pace along a narrow lane. The deep snow that lay undisturbed on the road before they slowed their progress.

Spying on the small group of fleeing peasants, he recalled Phu-Bar's standing orders to kill all who tried to leave the village without the sentor's permission. It was rumored that Laktos had many spies, and they were everywhere. Strict enforcement of the law was the only protection and was strongly encouraged.

Moleinar had the perfect reason to attack the unsuspecting families, and he wanted to torture and question them. If any of those who survived have knowledge of the bone man Laktos, he'd know about it soon enough.

He scrutinized the approaching group and counted nine men: six were walking two abreast in three columns, packing the snow as they went; a bedraggled horse followed closely behind, pulling a small, heavily laden wagon; one man was driving the rickety cart; and the last two were bringing up the rear with an occasional helping shove.

The wagon had its canvas sides rolled down in the frigid air. Moleinar guessed by the sounds of protest and whispered consolation from within that it held only defenseless women and children.

For the first time that day, Moleinar was beginning to see some good luck coming his way. In keeping with Apaula's plan, he needed witnesses to swear it was the army of Laktos that had slaughtered their loved ones. A woman and several children should do the trick. He would keep a couple of them alive, just in case. Then as soon as they were back in the township, he would let them escape, but only after he made sure they knew that the men who had slaughtered their friends and families were from the army of Laktos. Such shocking news carried on the lips of the simple-minded peasantry would spread like wildfire throughout the land. He smiled inwardly with just a hint of jealousy at the boldness of Apaula's plan.

He abruptly realized that he had an additional problem—what to do with them. He would have to hide the prisoners from Phu-Bar before he arrived, or the sentor would kill them himself. But who of the men that were with him now could he trust? It didn't take him long to decide. Scotty and his boyfriend Finnochio were the most obvious choices. Neither one of the two were very good fighters, but he thought they should be able to handle a young woman and a couple of squealing kids. Since they were also in on the plot to overthrow Phu-Bar, he could be certain of their silent cooperation. With the details now worked out, he needed only to act, for there was much to do and little time left. He formulated a simple plan of attack, then silently motioned for his men to get into position.

Phu-Bar let his soulless eyes roam over the scattered corpses as he barked out commands. "Drag those stinking bodies off that wagon and take them and those meat animals back to the village! Be sure to search the dead for anything of value. Mind you. Feed the meatier ones to the devil dogs and dump the remainder in the woods."

He dispassionately garnered every detail of the carnage that lay before him. He felt some inner satisfaction with the thoroughness of his minions and the abundance of death they had wrought here. It was unfortunate that he had missed the actual combat.

A shiver of intense pleasure, almost erotic in nature, passed through his rather large body. It began as a slight tickle from the tips of his pudgy feet and spread rapidly throughout his fleshy mass to his sparsely whiskered jowls, which promptly flushed a dark shade of crimson.

He inhaled the many putrid smells that wafted up from the human debris. As was his wont at times like this, he let his senses wander indiscriminately while he searched to identify each stale odor that teased his olfactory. The most predominate as usual was the scent of blood. He always found it interesting how the merest whiff left a pleasant metallic taste in his mouth.

Beneath the coppery aroma lay the pungent musk of fear and excrement—a deliciously sweet nectar that watered his taste buds with the flavor of triumph.

The cursing of several guards shattered his reverie, and all too quickly his rapture was replaced by his need for being here in this place. "Moleinar!"

The captain of the guard answered immediately from just a few feet behind him. "Here, sir."

"None of these people has been spared," Phu-Bar barked, gesturing angrily at the scattered corpses. "The women and children lay amidst the bodies of their husbands and fathers. It would seem the slaughter has been complete," Phu-Bar hissed, his voice laden with sarcasm.

Moleinar felt himself growing very nervous. "Yes, sir. As you ordered."

"So it would seem. Did I not also order you to question them?"

Moleinar felt his heart rate speed up. "Yes, and we did! I swear it!"

Phu-Bar spoke with a silky voice. "And what did you find out?"

Never before had Moleinar wished he were anyplace else than at that very moment. Even Apaula's disgusting presence would seem a joy compared to this. Reluctant to meet the sentor's gaze, his eyes fell on the body of a young woman cradling her baby protectively. It had served her to no avail evidenced by the spear that had pierced them both. A frozen pool of blood spread out beneath them changing the pristine white of the snow to a crystalline crimson that sparkled like a thousand ruby gems in the sunlight. He felt Phu-Bar's impatient eyes upon him and stammered out an answer. "There was one man who spoke of a group of people living in a secluded valley, sir."

Phu-Bar's interest was piqued. "What else did he say?"

"He said they passed through there late the day before as they fled and were welcomed by five men, two women and a small infant. They did not stay but passed through with only a brief stopover for water."

"Did they see him?"

"It was difficult to get a coherent answer from him between his sobs of anguish, but I thought that he said one of the men had been addressed as Laktos."

"Where exactly was this valley?"

Moleinar felt a lump form in his throat as he struggled with just how much information he should reveal. "He did not say," he answered feeling certain that Phu-Bar could see through his lie.

Phu-Bar remained outwardly unmoved by the disappointing news. But rage burned like the conflagrations of hell deep within the sentor's hateful orbs. Suddenly he reached out, grabbed the shorter man by the collar of his jerkin and pulled him to within an inch of his scraggly bearded face. "You will find the whereabouts of this Laktos," he spat out as if Laktos' name had left a foul taste

15

in his mouth. "I will have his hide, or I will see to it you never have children. Ever! Do you understand?!"

Moleinar nodded his head vigorously. "Yes, sir. Yes."

Phu-Bar glared in open disgust at Moleinar. "Send out more search groups! Send them to the four corners of the globe if you have to!"

The sentor shook Moleinar violently in sync with each booming word as he screamed, "Find this man and bring him back to me! Alive or dead! I don't care which!"

Phu-Bar dropped the cowering Moleinar, shoved him away, then spun on his heels and angrily strutted back toward the fortress. Woe to any who got in his way.

Moleinar watched him go with barely concealed hatred. "Soon, very soon, the taste of betrayal bittersweet," he said under his breath.

CHAPTER I

Three Months Later

In the vast emptiness of the cosmos, a not-too-distant star blazed in the cold black vacuum of space. The star had a name bestowed upon it by a race of beings that had once known it as Sol. Sol did not care about names or the species who gave them. It shone brightly as it had done since before humanity had conceived of time and long since after the day mankind had learned how to destroy himself.

The living sun gently caressed the world that was eternally held within its gravitational field. Its invisible streams of life generated energy, bringing warmth to the planet's atmosphere and nurturing all manner of life with its golden rays.

Above the world, scattered thunder clouds were loaded to bursting with airborne water vapor and floated lazily through cerulean tinted skies. The mountainous land beneath them was dappled in patterns of deep shadow and early morning light. A few of the clouds were unleashing a deluge of rain that turned the sky to a gray curtain of water beneath them.

The first beam of sunlight to celebrate the new day slipped up from beneath the horizon and spread its growing light across the land. Pure golden white beams of light reached out and touched the rain as it fell to the earth. The misty edges of the downpour captured the light rays and refracted them into the full visible spectrum. Vivid colors of red, orange, yellow, green, blue, indigo, and finally violet shone in stark contrast to the velvety dark background of the waning night. Dozens of rainbows arced across the sky, each with its own cloud island rising majestically above them. They appeared as magical castles supported on tremendous colored arches. Their size dwarfed the land beneath them and made the earth seem tiny by scale.

The last of the brightest stars eventually winked out as the world spun towards a new day. As the earth rotated upon its axis the sun rose higher in the sky. The sun's rays no longer sliced up from beneath the clouds, but now shone slightly downwards through them. A shifting patchwork quilt of light and shadow on the ground followed its movement above the few drifting clouds.

Far beneath those clouds was a sheltered valley, still mostly hidden in the shadow of the surrounding mountains. Across the valley a horizontal line of light descended slowly down the heavily treed western slope.

Winter was over by several weeks and spring had blossomed across this secluded dale, although the higher peaks still held a deep blanket of snow. Down in the meadow heavy dew covered a green silky carpet of rapidly growing wild hay grass. The cool morning air began to warm, kicking up a gentle breeze that circled the valley floor. The wind stroked the fields with invisible fingers, creating beautiful moving patterns in the copious growth.

Broad limbed majestic oak trees sparsely dotted the valley floor up to the base of the mountains that surrounded and enclosed the narrow refuge. The higher elevations were thickly carpeted in a forest of tall pines and bushy junipers.

A small clear creek brought icy cold water down from the lofty peaks as the warmer temperatures of spring melted the heavy winter snowpack.

Nestled down in the very center of the small valley was a modest farm. A small stone and log cottage and a slightly larger two-story barn were tucked away in a shaded orchard.

Behind the barn was a metal tub set up on a steel platform. A gated trough brought fresh water from the creek that kept the tub full. A similar sluice carried the overflow across the yard to the garden. The tub itself provided water for the corral and stable areas. It bordered up to the corral fence, which ran a hundred paces in a square.

A dirt path wound between the corral and the garden. Just beyond the garden, nestled in a grove of budding citrus trees, was the dwelling. A faint light flickered in the front window, yet all else was quiet about the house. Although no signs of life were immediately apparent within the humble cottage, there was an aura of expectation, a sense that the occupants would soon awaken.

It's not that the cottage was anything out of the ordinary as cottages went, but more that it had become an extension of the people who dwelled within it. It seemed as if it had absorbed the life force, the feelings and desires expressed by the inhabitants, and radiated it all outwards, back into the ether from whence it came.

Inside the cottage, the occupants slept blissfully comfortable, tucked away in their warm beds, all but one. Laktos floated through the ether world of his nightmares. He was helplessly ensnared in a web of buried memories that played out within the dreamscape of his subconscious mind.

He Dreamt of a Stranger

The presider was filled with abundant joy as he walked hand in hand through the village with his wife. The weather was perfect with just a hint of fall in the air. Today was the day he had planned for many months—today he would ask Lendura to be his wife.

The township was out in observance of the harvest festival, and everywhere he went people were laughing and rejoicing in celebration.

They followed a group of revelers along a winding lane through the thriving forest; the path was covered in amber fall leaves and dappled with splashes of sunlight. Clouds of perfumed incense filled the cool air with wonderful scents that floated upon a gentle breeze.

Artisans of all trades sold their wares from guild booths erected amid the trees on both sides of the cart-way; jewelry, pottery, wind chimes, incense, glass butterflies, leather masks, a plethora of fine craftsmanship were all in abundance.

Colorful streamers of cloth were draped by the hundreds from overhanging branches. They swayed in gentle rhythm to the hypnotic sound of dulcimer music that carried just above the joyous din of the crowd.

Lendura was like a child as she darted from merchant-to-merchant marveling at all the beautiful creations. An entourage of a half dozen chambermaids followed hurriedly in her wake their arms loaded with her purchases.

She ran to him, her face aglow with delight. She panted lightly as she gazed up at him smiling. Her upward glance chained him to silence. The stirring of the breeze brought him back to his senses. He sought to ask her to be his bride, but the words died upon his traitorous tongue.

"What is it, dear?" she asked quietly. Inside her heart skipped a beat, so strong was her longing for the one thing that she desired the most but dared not ask for—to rule and to have power over the people.

The presider appeared deep in thought. "Was it two years gone past that we met in this very spot?"

Lendura could barely whisper out her response, "Yes, dear." She cast her eyes demurely downward.

He hesitated, his face an unreadable mask. "This anniversary has given me the courage to speak thusly to you." Again, he paused.

Lendura felt certain that her heart would fly from her breast it fluttered so rapidly in anticipation of his proposal, for she was certain that's what he wished to ask. She knew this because Phu-Bar had told her of his friend's desire while they had sated a secret desire of their own late the night before.

She raised her head into the sunshine. Her dreamy eyes rested on the rolling foothills covered in acres of golden wildflowers basking in the late September air. She turned and looked expectantly at him while idly curling her hair around her index finger.

He mustered his courage to speak his heart but something in the back of his mind whispered, nagged at him to stop. An icy chill slid down the back of his neck, he felt as if someone watched him from afar and he turned to look.

He stood upon a low hill and gazed out over a bloody battlefield. Thousands of the dead and dying were strewn about him like scattered cords of wood. The bloody carnage was two to three bodies' deep in places and he could see that some of those bodies were incomplete.

In the distance he could see buildings and hear the faint sounds of laughter and music carried to him on a warm breeze. Standing on a small hillock just off to the side he spied a man and woman looking in his direction. They seemed vaguely familiar, as if he should know them, and yet upon careful scrutiny he did not recognize them at all.

His study of the couple was interrupted by something moving near his foot. Casually he looked down not really expecting anything other than some small scavenger gorging on the feast of dead. To his horror he saw a gore covered fist reaching up through layers of dismembered body parts. He stood paralyzed with disbelief as it groped around blindly searching for him. It touched his blood-soaked boot and clamped on.

An involuntary scream of revulsion escaped his lips as he tried to pull his foot free. To his surprise, his leg came up along with the hand and most of a forearm. He shook his leg trying to dislodge the grisly appendage, but it held firm with muscles it no longer possessed. It was squeezing so hard that his foot was hurting from the pressure.

Laktos pulled his sword from his scabbard and brought it down in an arc. "Let go of me!" The blade sliced cleanly through the knuckles of the hand severing all the fingers. The stump fell twitching to the ground. Severed fingers curled and flexed on the tip of his boot still vying for a good grip. He violently kicked them off.

No sooner had he rid himself of the unwanted digits when another hand grabbed his left ankle. And another followed by more until he was literally being pulled down by dozens of hands.

Panic gripped his heart as he frantically tried to break free, but his efforts proved futile. With horrifying swiftness, they pulled him beneath the writhing mass of bloody limbs.

He felt himself suffocating on their gore. He struggled to breathe.

Laktos bolted upright in bed with a gasp. His nightshirt was soaked with cold sweat and clung to his torso like a wet wrap. His heart raced in his chest for those first few seconds until he realized his surroundings.

It had all been a bad dream, but one so real that it had left him with a sensation of drowning that still haunted his mind. He unconsciously rubbed his chest, attempting to ease a pain in his lungs that shouldn't exist.

He tried to recall specifics from the nightmare, but the dream memory was quickly fading. There was something else just at the fringe of his mind, a brief flash of a man standing on a hilltop watching him. But even as he thought it, the memory dissipated like a wisp of smoke.

He struggled to piece together more of the elusive dream, but the harder he tried, the more uncertain he became of what had actually happened. He was still haunted frequently by visions or nightmares of a life that he might have lived in the distant past. His amnesia was complete as far as remembering anything past last year. He would give anything to be able to remember.

If not for the horrible dreams and his lack of a past, he would have total bliss in his life. He was in love with Inga in the here and now and that's all that was really important to him.

Inga slept peacefully beside him. Her face was turned upward haloed by her golden hair fanned out behind her head. He felt a warm swelling of love in his chest as he gazed down upon the child-like innocence of her sleeping form.

She Dreamt of Her Home

Inga ran up the slope to her house. Her pleated yellow skirt flew on the wind as she dashed toward home and her waiting family. Her bundle of schoolbooks she held tight to her small bosom as her skinny legs propelled her to the place she most wanted to be at that moment.

The cool smells of autumn hung over the hillsides. The grass was turning brown and all the trees were painted in vivid hues of oranges, yellows and reds. She loved the ones with the light-colored bark, almost white in appearance. They looked so pristine to her—so new with their bright changing leaves glistening in the late afternoon sun.

School was over for the winter and she felt a newfound freedom in her spirit. She beamed with youthful joy at thinking of the many long days ahead with nothing to do but to play with her friends.

She heard excited barking from up ahead just as Lucky flew over a small rise in the road and came tearing down the trail toward her at full speed. His little legs were a blur as they chewed up the distance between them. He had a sloppy look of dog happiness plastered on his scruffy face. His tongue hung halfway to the ground while his ears all but disappeared along the sides of his head. A dust trail followed in his tracks as he hurtled at Inga. She was forced to drop her books just in time to catch him as he leapt into her arms. Inga toppled over backwards into the tall grass at the edge of the road with Lucky frantically licking her face. She could feel the warm wetness of his sloppy kisses on her cheek.

Laktos leaned in close and gently kissed her rose-petal soft cheek. She smiled in her sleep and curled onto her side hugging his pillow to her bosom. He smiled contentedly then quietly slipped out from under the covers and crossed the room in near silence.

He dressed in his usual attire of loose-fitting dark cotton pants and a black billowing shirt secured around his waist with a wide brown leather belt. The belt was engraved with dragon heads and clasped with a cast jeweled pewter image of a swordsman fighting a serpent. From his belt hung a dagger and several fur pouches in which he carried gold coins and other everyday necessities. His shirt sleeves were bound at the wrists with black animal-hide bracers that laced up on the inside of the forearm. With his deer-hide boots in hand, he exited the tiny room.

As he entered the den, the sound of John's wheezing snore could be heard coming from behind a closed door to his left. Aside from the den and kitchen, it was the only other room in the tiny house.

The family area was to his front. It was barely fifteen feet on a side with two small diamond-paned windows flanking a stone fireplace. A dimly lit oil lantern sat upon the mantle. The flame was turned down so low that it flickered and waned constantly on the brink of extinction. He moved across the room and turned up the wick, watching as the tiny flame grew behind the glass housing until the room was brightened considerably.

Although the room was small, it held all of them comfortably during the worst days of winter. They had put a broad tree slab in the center of the room which served as their table. Around the table were five chairs and a short log bench set against the far wall. In the corner near the hearth was a small cradle.

Laktos recalled the moment when Sal had been inspired to make the rickety stick chairs by an alcohol-induced brainstorm of monumental proportions. To quote Sal, he'd had a "spontaneous exchange of drunken neurons that resulted in a mid-brain collision of thought energy that formed a rudimentary idea arrived at after several hours of liberal imbibing." Two blurry days later he had revealed his handiwork with Vespuccian pride and a definite slur.

The handmade seats were an unsightly tangle of protruding twigs and branches intertwined together with fall leaves still clinging to dormant buds and thus bent into the vague shape of a chair. Now that winter had ebbed, it appeared as though two chairs had actually started to sprout leaves. Laktos speculated whether they would grow into more chairs or just make themselves bushier. How Sal had put the shrub-like furniture together was not as great a mystery as what was keeping them together. By some Vespuccian miracle, and a lot of gingerly placed buttocks, none had broken—yet.

Laktos figured it couldn't possibly be much longer before someone's chair collapsed. He smiled thinking about a stormy winter's night not so long ago when they had all teased Sal about his carpentry skills. Sal had taken the gibing with good humor and had even started a gamblers' pot for the first victim of his hobbled-together craftsmanship.

Laktos laid a couple of logs on the still-glowing embers of the previous night's fire and stoked it back to life. He stood in front of the hearth and stared blankly into the flames letting the warmth and dancing lights mesmerize and calm him while his thoughts continued to meander aimlessly. His mind flooded with happy memories from many a stormy day sitting together around that stump playing games and sharing stories of the baffling adventure called life.

This line of thinking inevitably led him to pondering about his own life and the circumstances for his existence. Mostly he thought about his quest for the answers to those questions that still haunted him. The evil wizard Drang had revealed a portion of his lost past to him, but it seemed the more he discovered the more he realized how little he really knew. And what of the cost to learn what he had. Losing Yennek and the other crewman, the sinking of the Morning Star, and all the suffering they had all endured hardly felt worth the scant rewards. The self-knowledge that he had sought on Monad's island was more elusive now than ever before and worse, he now carried the burden of the demise of the others as if it were his own hand that had caused their deaths.

Inga had reminded him frequently that they had all chosen of their own accord to follow Laktos on his quest knowing full well the dangers involved. It was foolhardy for him to take the blame himself and she would allow him no self-pity. Her loving rebuke had eased his anguish, but only slightly.

More worrisome to him was their uncertain future and the pain it would bring. He kept these thoughts to himself. The last several months had been the happiest he had felt since his mysterious arrival in this place nearly a year before and he feared saying anything that would dampen that feeling.

Even though he did not voice them, his fears about the near future were always on his mind, for he could feel the inescapable wind of fate that was just beginning to blow outside his window. And there was nowhere to seek shelter from the coming storm.

Above the fireplace on the mantle lay several of Inga's inventions. It was one of these that he focused on engaging his attention as a distraction from that other stream of thinking.

Laktos reached to the shelf and picked up a piece of cloth about two feet in length with tiny holes perforated precisely along carefully measured marks. Each mark bore a number starting with the lowest digit at the bottom of the strip and counting upwards to twelve. He stretched it out upright and lined up one hole on the lantern and studied the strip. "Amazing," he breathed. Inga's ability to invent new and mind-boggling things from her overactive imagination constantly astounded him. Her insight seemed more magical than logical to him and yet her devices always worked. In his spread hands he held a simple cloth that measured the distance between the earth and the sun in order to tell the time of day. Thinking about the time gave him a sudden urge to stop lamenting and get on about his day. He neatly rolled the solar measuring cloth into a ball and placed it back on the mantle.

He pulled on his boots, laced up the sides, then turned toward the front door. In two steps he passed an ancient reflecting glass that hung upon the wall to his left. His reflection momentarily caught his eye. He stopped and studied the image that gazed back at him.

He stood six feet in height with a lean muscular physique that weighed about two hundred pounds. His shoulder length black hair had receded from his temples and had more gray in it since the last time he'd bothered to take notice, as did his lengthening beard. Sometimes when he looked into the old, faded mirror, he felt as if it were a stranger glaring back at him. It was an eerie, otherworldly feeling that reminded him of his experience deep within the building on Monad's island.

There, he had walked upon the feet of his reflection in the great hall. When he had gazed down into his own face and met the questioning eyes of his doppelganger looking back from the depths of the polished emerald floor, there had been a moment when he wasn't sure which of them was the real Laktos. It seemed his world had flipped upside down and he was gawking upwards at himself. Now, just like then, his reflected image stared back at him and he wondered what life was like inside the looking glass. After his experience with the portals, it was easy to imagine that he looked into a doorway rather than at a reflection.

He moved in closer to the mirror until his breath fogged the glass then gazed deep into his own eyes. It was strange how his reflection did not look as he expected himself to appear. "Who are you really?" He searched the hazel-green orbs that stared back at him for an answer but felt no connection to the reflected image. He thought about the wizard Drang's obscure revelation concerning his dreams and how they held the key to his past, knowledge that had aged him in ways that didn't show outwardly. Sometimes he would awaken from a troubled sleep with a weariness that pulled at his heart and would not let him forget some terrible loss—a feeling of deep sadness for which there seemed but one explanation—the past life that Drang had shown him might have been real, not just a fantasy created by his imagination to fill in the blank pages of his missing memory.

He stared a moment longer, as if he expected to see his reflection shrug or perhaps answer him with some sage advice, but his mirrored image remained mute. He felt slightly uncomfortable with the silence. "I thought you'd say that," he whispered as he turned away and went outside the front door.

The morning air was crisp with a cold freshness that revitalized his spirit and invigorated his body. He stretched and took in several deep breaths as he greeted the rising sun just beginning to crest the mountaintops in the east. He felt his spirit recharged on the bounty of nature as he turned and made his way toward the barn and his sleeping friends.

"Perhaps I should not worry so much about the past, when right now is where I am," he thought idly. He found himself having this internal argument more and more frequently as of late. His desire for the truth sometimes kept him rooted in a past that he could not fully remember. What he could remember was intertwined with Drang's revelations so tightly that he could no longer be certain of what was really true. The doubts that he had only served to fuel his uncertainty and left him feeling adrift in life with no foundation on which to hold on to. Was his past that important?

More disturbing as of late was the constant effort of self-control he needed in order to stay focused on the bounty of love and friendship that was with him now and to stop dwelling on that which he could not find. Yet the mystery of those missing years haunted him. It seemed he was only half alive without a remembered past.

To his left behind a split log rail fence across mist-covered fields he could see a small herd of beefalo grazing contentedly. John, Sal and he had rounded up the small herd last fall and succeeded in corralling them. The fresh milk they provided was a godsend for Sienna and Little John, her infant son, along with the necessary meat that had sustained them throughout the harshest days of winter past.

To his right was the garden. Sal had worked a miracle of growth and the fruits of his labors were becoming obvious. The small family of friends would soon benefit from Sal's efforts. The bags of seed that they discovered in the back of the barn were proving fertile as tomatoes, bell peppers, cucumbers, squash, carrots, cantaloupes, corn and a variety of beans and peas all vying for more space as they grew in rampant abundance in the spring weather.

Sal showed a natural talent and passion for horticulture. He would often spend his entire afternoon working this little plot of land to keep it free of weeds and insects. More than once he had come in from the small field with his palms stained green and his fingernails black from digging in the dirt. Inga teased him when she said that it was his green thumb that caused everything to flourish so heartily.

Laktos casually approached the barn doors. He grasped a large iron ring and pulled open the left entry door. From way in the back came the thunderous sound of multiple snores. He wondered how anyone could sleep through the terrible noise, but somehow it seemed not to bother the four slumbering inhabitants within. He stepped inside the threshold and beheld his friends all curled up together near the back of the stables. Sunlight streamed past him and cast his larger-than-life shadow into the building.

Sal, Captain Caruso and Raziel lay with their heads perched on Prometheus the dragon and his rather round stomach. Their heads rose and fell in gentle rhythm with each breath the dragon took. Prometheus lay curled on his side with his tail protectively wrapped across their prone forms. The four of them snored in perfect unison.

Laktos was continually amazed at the wonder of their friendship and the mysterious journey that had brought them all together. He cherished these simple moments and knew he must revel in them, for nothing lasted forever. Deep in the recesses of his consciousness he felt as if he stood upon the precipice of time and no matter how hard he tried to ignore the feeling; he somehow knew these days of innocent simplicity were coming to an end.

His friends looked so peaceful that he decided not to rouse them just yet. He turned away, went back outside, and around the side of the barn to the wash basin. They made it from an old steel tank about ten feet across the middle and three feet deep. An iron frame which was mounted a-foot-and-a-half above the ground supported it. Beneath the tank was a fire pit they had used in the winter months to heat the water for the women and the baby. A series of wooden troughs brought water from the nearby creek into the tub, which kept it constantly full of fresh, cold water. He dipped his hands into the icy bath and washed the slumber from his face.

Sienna was awakened by something wriggling and squirming next to her in bed. She opened her eyes and saw her son sucking his tiny thumb as he stared back at her with stern, sapphire green eyes. Sienna could already see the resemblance to his father, and the thought made her smile broadly. She tickled his little round belly until his frown turned into a smile of delight. John giggled and laughed, all the while kicking his feet and trying to brush her poking fingers away with his wee arms.

"Whoops," Sienna said. "It seems I tickled the pee right out of you." She quickly picked up the baby and held him away from the bed as his diaper cloth leaked urine down his leg. "It's for certain that I'll be mopping the floor this morn. No thanks to you, little man."

She kissed his cheek as she laid him on her drawer stack and cleaned him up. She bathed him, then dressed him in clean linens. He fussed and grumped the whole time.

"I know you're hungry. Stop squirming about before you get stuck with this pin. Ouch!" She cursed under her breath as her finger throbbed with pain. She finally got the pin fastened without impaling Little John, or herself anymore, and raised him to her bosom.

The young boy greedily took to her nipple and suckled noisily as if to say, "It's about time."

Sometime later, she placed him over her shoulder and gently patted his back until he belched. "Now, aren't you the well-mannered gentleman. You're just like your father."

She tickled him again but thought it might be better if she didn't. "Come on, then. It's time for me to eat or there won't be anything left of me to feed you."

She cradled him in her arms and walked to the den. Across the room near the fireplace was John's cradle. Sienna gently laid him in it and covered him with a thin blanket. She sat on the fireplace stoop next to him and slowly rocked the cradle, letting her mind wander as she watched him nod off to sleep. He didn't have a care in the world. Thankfully, he didn't even know that he differed from other children, at least not yet. But that would all change as he got older and his physical deformities became more obvious. Sadly, she prayed he would live that long as she continued to rock him gently to sleep.

Inga Still Lay Sleeping

She was running across a pasture of knee-high grass. The air was warm and held all the promises of spring. The vivid green grassland sparkled with dew drops in the bright sunlight. Her dog Lucky ran along next to her, barking excitedly with joy. His brown eyes gleamed with happiness and a big sloppy grin spread across his furry face. She could hear Laktos laughing and sharing her joy, and she could sense the warmth of his presence nearby, but she never actually saw him. It was as if she were so comfortable with him around that she no longer saw him as a person with feelings or maybe that life together had become so routine that the years felt as though they were all planned out, and the idea of that scared her just a little.

In the distance, she could see the house. Her house since she was too young to remember. She had always been here and always would. She felt a sense of completeness knowing that her mama and papa were waiting for her inside.

Suddenly she was there at the house standing on the front porch looking back across the fields. Tears streamed down her cheeks as she succumbed to a great sorrow. Somehow the colors of the sky and the fields seemed different. She could see the sun overhead without a cloud in the sky and yet there was a dimness to the entire scene that made it look lifeless. The world had turned dark somehow as if the bright sunny morning had been replaced by a cloudy afternoon. It was then that she noticed that Lucky had disappeared. In a panic she spun around searching for him. She turned around and faced herself. "Your feelings are the most important right now. Don't even think about what's happened—just come home."

She blinked and now she sat immobile—her body devoid of any sign of life except for her emotionless eyes. She sat in the center seat of a ship dory staring at a night-shrouded, rain-swept shoreline. Lightning flashed, and for that brief second, she could see a rope that led from the bow of the small boat up to a figure waving frantically at her from the water's edge.

Around her raged a terrible storm, and although her boat was tossed about, she sat unfazed by the turmoil that engulfed her. She was an island adrift in the eye of the storm.

She could see that he was yelling to her, trying to tell her something. His gestures appeared to be frantic, his crying pleas echoed between the pounding surf as he struggled to pull in the slack on the rope. Still, she sat, empty of all feelings, just watching as if it were a play and she merely a spectator.

His voice resonated with desperation between the booming thunderclaps. She couldn't hear him over the roar of the surf. And besides, it just did not seem important. Idly she felt it was odd that she had no emotion for the man, as if something inside her had died and she just wasn't willing to try to get it back or whether she even could—she felt empty inside.

The sea grew rougher and waves tossed the little craft in every direction except towards the shore and safety. The rope disappeared into the black frothing water, and just when she thought her lifeline had been severed, it would pull taught in the troughs and vibrate with the extreme effort that the figure on shore was exerting in trying to pull her back. A fraction of a sentence was carried across the wind-swept waves: "Inga. Come baaa—I love you—" She realized with a start that the man on the beach was Laktos. At that moment, the rope snapped with a fierce jerk and the parted end whipped past her head trailing a spray of water. She could feel its passing wind. The dory immediately floated farther out to sea.

Inga sat unmoved by the vision of Laktos throwing himself into the turbulent waves again and again only to be thrust violently back upon the rocks of the beach with each hopeless attempt to reach her. His body was torn to shreds of flesh by the unforgiving rocks as he continued to beg for her return, but his pleas served him to no avail.

She drifted farther out to sea with every beat of her heart and further away from the man that she had sworn to love forever. Curiously, she felt no sense of loss or fear, just an emptiness where her heart should have been.

His anguished cry pierced the storm that raged around her, the aching wail in his voice one of utter despair and insufferable loss. "Inga!"

Laktos faded into the storm and she could no longer see the beach through the pouring rain. Carried by the unforgiving currents of time, she floated away as if they had never been—going home.

Inga sat up from her nightmare with a startled gasp. Immediately, she reached out for Laktos, but the bed was empty. Momentary panic gripped her heart like a vise until she vaguely remembered a kiss and felt that he was somewhere nearby, probably outside waking up the others.

She slipped her feet out from under the covers and hurried across the cold floor over to her dresser. As she dressed, she thought about her dream and what it could mean. The only really clear memory she could recall from the dream was a strong desire to return home. Inga felt a pang of homesickness as she thought about her mama and papa, so far away. She wondered if they were all right, if they were worried about her. Inga realized with a sense of dread that if she stayed here, she might never see them again. A feeling of momentary anxiety gripped her heart, and she suddenly felt the distance between herself and home. It seemed impossible that she had come so far across the globe. Even if she left today, which of course she couldn't if Laktos didn't want to go along, still it would take them months to reach the shores of Sweadon. Maybe, she thought, Laktos would choose to go. There wasn't any real reason for them to stay here. If she presented the idea to him as a grand adventure, he probably would jump at the opportunity.

He wouldn't admit it to her, but she could see that he was becoming more restless with each passing day. The sedate life of a farmer did not suit him—it was as if he were destined for greater deeds and merely biding his time in this place.

After several minutes of silent debate, she came to a decision about the issue and resolved to discuss it with Laktos before the day ended.

She dressed in her prettiest turquoise skirt with a flowered bodice over a sky-blue, loose-sleeved blouse. She gazed at herself in the looking glass next to her dresser as she carefully clasped a tiny gold cross on a delicate matching chain around her neck. Satisfied with her appearance, she walked out of the room.

"Good morning," Inga said softly as she entered the common room, still adjusting her clothing. Seeing that Sienna was rocking Little John off to sleep she padded into the kitchen and began quietly taking dishes and pans out of the cupboards in preparation to cook.

Sienna came in a few moments later and lent a hand. Inga could tell by Sienna's expression that something was bothering her, and she had a good idea what it might be. "Worrying about Little John?"

Sienna opened up a wellspring of emotions. "If only we had found Capernaum." She rambled on, just speaking without really thinking about what she said. "I don't even know if there is such a place. Now it all seems so hopeless. John and I placed all our hopes for the baby on a stupid legend." She sobbed.

Inga put her arm around Sienna's shoulder. "You mustn't lose faith. Something good will happen. I just know it."

Sienna gazed into Inga's eyes and took comfort from her friend. "I hope you're right. I couldn't live without my son."

"Tell me about this Capernaum place. What is it? A city?"

"John and I grew up in a small village where most of the people believed in the myths and stories of the Ancients. I always thought that they were dumb to believe in such nonsense, but I never spoke of it out loud for fear of retribution."

"Strange how people turn on each other when they don't believe in the same things," Inga mused. She encouraged Sienna to keep speaking as she puttered around the kitchen preparing their morning meal.

Sienna's talk of home made Inga think of her dream again and of her own parents that she had left behind a long time ago. She had been missing them a lot lately and secretly desired to go back to Sweadon someday, soon. It would be good to see the family. She was still trying to figure out how to break the news to Laktos.

"That all changed when I met John," Sienna said, lost in the memory. "He was the son of the town's only butcher and I would see him several times a week when he delivered meat to my aged mother. As time passed, we became friends and then lovers." Sienna blushed, "He delivered meat to me every day."

Inga smiled knowingly, encouraging her to continue.

"Then one day he showed up on our doorstep with an old book with strange words and drawings in it. He'd said that he'd discovered it a few years back in a locked trunk stored in the attic of his father's shop."

"Where did it come from?" Inga asked as she diced up another potato and added it to the stew pot.

"No one knows. He asked his father, but he swore that he'd never seen it before."

"That's strange. What was in the book? What did it say?"

"Near as we could understand, it talked about a man who came here from a village called Haven or Heave. Something like that. The words were badly faded. His father sent him to rescue some people who had gotten lost in the world."

"It sounds very intriguing. Was this a true story? Did the man ever find the people he sought?"

"We aren't sure. Most of the pages had been torn out and what was left was in terrible condition and difficult to read. What we could get from the story was that this man could heal the sick and dwelled in a place called Capernaum for a time."

"That's the name you mentioned earlier."

"It's a city founded by the ancient gods according to the old legends. Supposedly it still exists somewhere to the north of here."

"Is that why you and John left your home? To seek this place and a cure for your child?"

Sienna frowned as she replied. "I know now that it was foolish to believe in such nonsense, but in the town where we came from, children misshapen as my baby was were put to death. We just didn't have any other hope, but now I see it was always hopeless."

"No. No, it's not a fool's errand," Inga consoled. "You said yourself that it may be true what the old book says."

"That's why it's hopeless."

"I don't understand."

"Because the old book says that the same man who is supposed to live in Capernaum and can cure my son was murdered by those who he was sent to save."

"Murdered! That makes little sense. Why would the people who he healed kill him?"

"I don't know," Sienna said with a sigh. "The book was confusing and hard to understand. What I could make out was that he was tortured and killed for teaching people how to love his father."

Inga was silent for a moment as she thought about Sienna's words. When she spoke, it was in solemn tones. "In my travels I have seen the cruelty that men inflict upon themselves, and at those times I wondered if I really belonged to the human race." She saw the questioning look in Sienna's eyes. "I guess what I'm trying to say is that I've never understood how a person could treat another as if they had the right to control their destiny. That privilege lies with God and no mortal creature should be permitted or able to wield God's power on this earth."

"If only it were so," Sienna whispered. "If only."

Inga stopped what she was doing and gave Sienna a warm hug of encouragement. "Not all men are evil. John is a good man with a loving heart. You could not ask for more."

"Yes, I suppose that you're right." Sienna paused. "I sometimes forget that we are blessed to be with men such as these. I see a kindred spirit in all of them which is probably why they're all such good friends."

"There's a bond between them that I do not comprehend, and I think that no woman probably could. Sometimes when they speak to each other I feel as if there's a whole other conversation taking place that I am only peripherally aware of."

"Isn't that the truth." A hint of loving exasperation crept into Sienna's voice which immediately had the two women smiling with the shared bond of their experience.

Almost in unison they said, "Men—can't live with them, can't live without them."

Laughing they split apart. Sienna helped set the table and Inga went back to her cooking. She silently searched her heart for the answer to the one question that had preoccupied her mind lately—could she live without Laktos if he chose not to come with her back to her homeland as she had been contemplating?

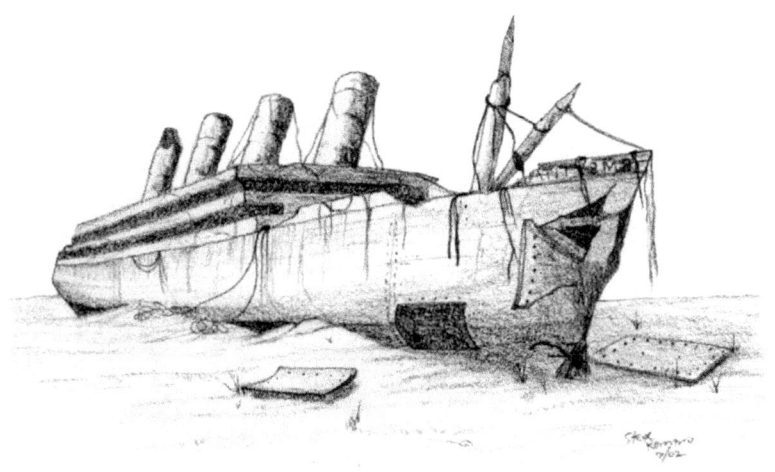

50

Chapter 2

Laktos let his gaze wander around the valley as he drank in the beauty of his surroundings. They were all truly blessed to live in such a fertile place. He had been to the desolate places. He recalled the dried sea bed with the rusting hulk of the Ancients' ship lying on its side in the sunbaked, cracked earth. The memory of it made him appreciate their bountiful valley all the more.

Eventually his eyes fell upon the forge that he and John had recently constructed. With this recent addition to the farm, they could now fashion iron into shovels, plows, scythes and many other useful tools to make their farm work a little easier. They would have to plan a trip to the old ruins and see if they could scrounge some metal now that the roads had become passable again.

Three hens clucked their way past Laktos. Unconcerned by his presence, they bobbed and strutted their way over to the corral and scratched in the dirt for grubs. He noticed their feathers needed clipping again to prevent them from joining the flocks of wild chickens that flew overhead on almost a daily basis.

Laktos had a pretty good idea that John was up and moving about as it was John's habit to let the chickens out of their coop each morning on his way to the outhouse.

Laktos leaned on the fence rail and absently watched the chickens as he patiently waited for the day's routine to begin again. A short time later, the smell of wood smoke and cooking food wafted from the cottage chimney and settled over the farm. Somewhere beyond the house their only rooster crowed in anticipation of the burgeoning day.

John came around the corner of the house still tying the drawstring on his breeches as he walked over to Laktos. "Good morning, Laktos." John stepped up beside him and leaned his forearms casually on the fence.

"Morning, John. Looks like it's going to be another beautiful day."

"Fine with me. I've had enough of cold weather for a while," John said as he rubbed his right knee.

"That limb still bothering you? How long has it been since the attack?"

"Almost an entire season now."

"Is that all? So much has happened that sometimes it feels as if it's been years since we first met."

"I know what you mean," John agreed. "This time last year my only hope had been to find a cure for my son. I had no idea where I would be living or who I would meet along my journey. It's almost scary the way things have all turned out. I mean if you hadn't saved me and my family on that day we first met, then I wouldn't have been there those many weeks later to rescue Inga and your friends."

Laktos nodded. "Strange, isn't it? Life and the way things happen for reasons we can never decipher. Nothing matters until the moments we choose are taken. And once taken, that choice is irretrievably gone to a past we cannot alter. From that moment forward we can only pray that we have made the right choices." Laktos said somberly. "I shudder to think of what may have become of Inga had I not saved your life."

"Fortunately, we will never have to find out," John said with a smile.

A comfortable silence settled over the two men as they each remained lost in their own thoughts, absently watching the beefalo graze. John looked skyward. "I remember when we sat by the fire that first night and talked about the mysteries of the Ancients. I thought they were fairytales told to keep naughty children in bed at night," he chuckled sadly. "I could never have imagined that it all might have been true sometime in the distant past." John turned his gaze to Laktos. "Tell me again about the old city of the Ancients that you found. What was it like?"

Laktos didn't answer him at first. He looked to the heavens and watched as a single bright speck of light arced steadily across the sky. "There." He pointed at the speck. "We watched that same light all those many months ago, and we talked about the Ancients who might dwell upon them."

"I remember. We thought of them as gods."

"Yes, we did. Didn't we? But the truth is even more unbelievable and heartbreaking. If only they had been gods. Then we could distance ourselves from the horror of their deeds. But they were not deities—they were men like you and me. They were our ancestors, and they destroyed their world, our world, for the want of power and glory.

I've been to their lifeless city and marveled at the wonders that they had created, but all their wondrous devices were for naught. Nothing remained of the inhabitants except their rag-shrouded corpses piled in the streets." Laktos stopped speaking. The memory of his encounter with MOT and the knowledge that the librarian had shown him was almost too great to bear alone, yet he dared not speak of it to anyone. Not even Inga knew the whole truth of his encounter with MOT. "This is our legacy—to live on the ashes of our forefathers."

"But wasn't there still something of value, of use to us in the old place?" John speculated. "I mean. If the portals still work, isn't it possible that other devices may still function? Imagine what we could accomplish—"

"No!" Laktos spouted out, immediately regretting the fact that he cut John off rather abruptly. In a quieter tone he continued. "What would we gain by following in the footsteps of those who perished before us but a similar fate?"

John saw a great sadness creep into his friend's eyes and was sorry for asking him about his encounters. After a brief silence he tactfully changed the subject. "I don't know about you, but my stomach is growling with hunger and those delicious smells coming from the house are only making it worse. Come on. Let's get some chow and leave this somber talk for another day."

Laktos' thoughts were far away as he responded. "Sounds like a good idea." He turned his head and looked at John. A smile slowly replaced the worried frown that had been his mask moments before. With little more than a hint of facetiousness he asked, "Should we wake the others or just let them sleep through breakfast?"

John grinned as he spoke in kind. "You know Sal would never forgive you if you let him miss a meal."

"Not to mention the captain and Raziel," Laktos added with mock sternness and a twinkle in his eye.

"I wouldn't want to disturb their dreams," John quipped.

"Of course not!" Laktos said with feigned indignation. "Especially Prometheus."

John looked serious for a fleeting second. "Do dragons really dream?"

"Of course they do," Laktos admonished. "They just call it something else."

Chapter 3

Prometheus Dreamed of Gliding Through the Heavens

He had never felt such happiness before. Every sensation seemed brand new. Playfully he darted in and out of white, cottony clouds that floated serenely through the crisp, clear sky. He spied movement and looked down to see his love mate Pallas circling a thousand claws below him. She hadn't yet seen him, so he was content to watch as she teasingly chased a flock of wild chickens across the sky. She was his new hope for living after all his decades of loneliness. He had nearly given up hope of ever finding another of his kind, let alone one that he could love so deeply. He had found new joy in living, flying and playing with her. His life had new found meaning for him, as if he'd been reborn.

He spread his wings and dove towards her. He swooped in beside her and together they scattered the flock. The temporarily frightened birds reformed their flock a short distance away and continued off into the distance.

Bored with the birds, he dove towards the earth from the hovering clouds. The winds whistled past his ears as he plummeted straight down as if to say, "Look what I can do!"

Gleefully, she raced earthward after him. Her slim neck stretched out gracefully, streamlining her form as she closed the gap between them.

He waited until the last possible moment, then spread out his wings and leveled off just over the treetops. He misjudged his speed and clumsily his tail shredded the leaves off several treetops. His velocity dropped off dramatically.

Pallas was right behind him and closing fast. She pulled out of her dive a second before he did and swished by over his head to take the lead. He could feel the wind turbulence from her as she arrowed past.

He drove himself harder to catch up as she looked back at him and teased him with her eyes. His larger wing span closed the distance. He watched her as she flew just ahead and slightly beneath him. He admired the beauty of her body and the way her muscles moved beneath the bright sheen of her scales. The way she used her tail as a delicate balance to the beating of her wings was the perfect symmetry of beauty to him. He knew he was hopelessly in love with her and would never desire another for the rest of his life.

He arced into a high bank turn and closed the distance a little more. Something in the forest not far in front of her glinted brightly in the sun. He turned his attention on the bright object. His heart skipped a beat as he realized what it could mean. Pallas was headed straight for trouble.

She glanced back to see her love trying frantically to reach her. Pallas floated along, not as determined to win but wanting more to be caught by her lover. She teased him with a smile, only just beginning to sense that his aura was troubled. She did not see the catapult launch, its deadly spear with unerring accuracy. She barely felt the razor-sharp tip as it pierced her breast and pulled her from the sky.

"NOOO!" Prometheus thought.

He swooped down beneath her falling body in an attempt to save her from a fatal impact. Together, they crashed through the treetops accompanied by the sound of snapping branches and crushed foliage to land on the forest floor with a loud thump. Prometheus was covered with numerous scratches and scrapes. Blood oozed from dozens of small wounds. He felt none of them as he crawled over to where Pallas lay. She was sprawled on her back with the spear shaft protruding from her chest, its bronze base pointing toward the heavens. Ever so gently, he laid his wing across her unmoving body.

He carefully put his muzzle close to hers and looked into her open eyes. "Pallas?" he could barely say her name. "Pallas, my love." Tears welled up in his eyes as he sensed the awful truth. He kissed the lids of her beautiful brown and gold eyes that he loved so much and tenderly closed them for the last time.

He lay frozen in shock and disbelief at the sudden turn of events. Absently, he saw the delicate curve of her jaw through the haze of his unshed tears. He saw the way her brow ridge tapered around to her petite ears and the way her scales shimmered in the waning light of day. He took all this in as if he were standing apart and watching it all happen to someone else.

But the shimmer was fading and her nostrils did not pass air any longer. Beneath his wing, he could feel the beat of her heart no more. He knew at that moment that his beloved was gone from him forever. His soul cried out in agony as his tears flowed freely from grief-filled eyes. Each soul tormented drop instantly turned to crystal as they fell unrestrained to the blood stained earth.

Sometime later his grief was interrupted by the shouts of many men searching through the forest for their prize kill. Prometheus' heartbreak flared into unbounded hatred for the humans. With a last kiss, he left his beloved's lifeless body behind and went in search of his revenge.

Prometheus' eyes burned with bloodlust as he scanned the woods passing beneath. He spotted the murderers crossing a small glade just ahead. Six men were spread out in a semicircle as they marched slowly across the meadow, clad in their bulky suits of metal armor. Behind them followed four horses tended by three rag-clothed peasants, all of which pulled and pushed their huge killing machine across the open field.

Prometheus turned and swooped down from above.

Sal was shoved violently by the still sleeping Prometheus.

"Merda! Son of a pig!" he muttered, still not fully awake. He sat up and looked around to see who had tossed him about. Prometheus moaned behind him. Still caught up in his nightmare, he thrashed about more aggressively.

"What in blazes—?" Caruso's waking question was abruptly cut short as Prometheus' tail whipped up and sent him flying into Raziel. He sputtered out a loud grunt as he collided with the sleeping man. The two men rolled several feet away and came to a stop entangled together in a human pretzel knot.

"What just happened?" a confused Raziel groaned. He untangled himself from the captain and stood up and dusted himself off. "Anyone see the wagon that just ran me into the dirt—look out!" Prometheus slashed at the air with his talons. Sal's eyes opened wide in horror as he saw an enormous claw swinging towards his head. Acting on reflex, he ducked and leapt. He felt the air move behind his head and knew that the strike had been very close. He tucked and rolled upon landing and crashed head-on into the other two just standing up. All three went crashing down to end sprawled face up just inside the open doorway to the barn.

John and Laktos were still debating whether or not to wake their friends when they heard confused shouts coming from the barn. They both stopped and listened for a moment while looking questioningly at each other. Another shout rang out.

"Come on! Something's wrong," Laktos spat out with urgency. He turned and ran towards the barn with John close on his heels. They rounded the corner of the building and dashed inside only to run headlong into the other three laid out on the floor.

Prometheus soared down on them while they were exposed in the open field. He came at them with the sun to his back and let loose a deadly stream of fire in their midst.

"What the—" Laktos looked past the grumbling party to see Prometheus moaning and thrashing about in his sleep. He could see that his friend was suffering from a nightmare. He turned to the others. "It looks like he's having a dream-haunt."

"Oh, that's what you call it!" Raziel snapped as he rubbed at a sore knee.

"I should have asked him to wake you with a kiss," Sal mocked as he puffed out his lips and made smooching sounds at Raziel.

Raziel glared back at him, but before he could speak, the captain interrupted their irritating banter.

"Stow it, you two bilge-rats. This looks serious. Is there anything that we can do, Laktos?" There was genuine concern in Caruso's voice and pleading in his eyes.

Laktos answered after a few seconds of musing. "Yes. I'm going to try to reach him. If I can make contact, I may be able to wake him from his nightmare." He didn't wait for approval from them; he knew what he needed to do. Laktos moved deeper into the barn and crept closer to his dragon friend. The others watched in nervous silence.

His first pass took out the catapult and the slaves. He circled around for another strike. The bold knights were fleeing towards the protection of the forest. He wheeled around and cut a path across theirs. He incinerated four of them with a single breath.

The remaining humans screamed in fear and agony as they tried to flee his wrath. He dove down at them once more. His hatred for them burned with a heat that stifled the flames from their burning bodies. He attacked again and again. He exhaled his anger and pain with each burning breath letting his grief fuel his murderous rage until their bodies had long since burned to dust and their metal suits had melted to slag.

Laktos barely avoided getting his arm chopped off twice by snapping jaws. On his third attempt, he made contact with Prometheus' scaly hide just behind his right eye. Their thoughts were immediately intertwined and Laktos viewed Prometheus' dream as if he were a part of it.

When he was done, nothing moved in the meadow. All that remained were smoldering piles of ashes and a few bones. He landed amidst the carnage and picked up a leg bone in his mouth. He crushed it in his jaws and spit out the fragments in disgust. His hatred for humans consumed his every thought for a long time. When his need for revenge was sated, his anger was replaced with a feeling of nearly overwhelming emptiness. He took no pleasure from the death of the humans—only the certain knowledge that they would kill no more of his kind.

He returned to Pallas' remains and wept beside her still form until all his tears had been shed and his eyes went dry. His heart felt like a lead weight in his chest that would crush his spirit. "If only it would," he thought. "So I could be with you once again, Pallas, my love." He felt a bottomless well of solitude and emptiness open in his soul that he knew he could never fill. His will to live abandoned him. He somberly turned away from her corpse. His only desire was to rejoin his own kind until his imminent death.

"Prometheus." Laktos felt as if he were whispering, but how could he really know his tone when he never actually uttered a word out loud. "Wake up. It's me, Laktos."

Prometheus heard his name called as if from a great distance. He wasn't sure if he really heard it or not. His mind was drifting between two worlds and his emotions were still very much tied to the horrific dream—much too aware of that last moment with Pallas.

"Prometheus. Wake up. It's me. Laktos." He tried to think a little louder, but wasn't exactly sure how to go about doing it. "Wake up, old friend. There is nothing to fear in this place."

Laktos felt the dragon stir beneath his touch at the same moment he felt the mental awareness of Prometheus' waking mind. He also sensed the pain and anguish that his friend was experiencing. "Are you all right?" he asked. His concern touched Prometheus' heart, helping ease his pain.

Prometheus lay absolutely motionless on the straw floor. His breathing had slowed and he no longer thrashed about.

The others, gathered nearby, watched in numbed silence as Laktos quieted their friend with his touch. Laktos knelt near the dragon with his eyes closed. His left hand lay comfortingly on Prometheus' neck.

"Laktos," Prometheus uttered tersely. He struggled with his dream rage and fought an inner battle with his desire to kill all humans. Through his strength of will, he reminded himself that these humans were his friends and that he owed his life to Laktos. He let go a heavy sigh and all the force of his nightmare drained away from his soul with the exhaled breath. He knew what he had to do.

Laktos felt an inner peace settle over his friend and knew that the worst had passed. He understood from his own experience how difficult it was sometimes to adjust to a waking reality when the dream realm seemed just as real. His own dreams were often in the realm of nightmares, reliving past events that he could not remember in the light of day.

"Laktos. I'm glad that you're here." Prometheus opened his eyes but did not raise his head. With one eye he looked towards the opened door and saw John, Raziel, Sal and Captain Caruso gazing back at him. He twisted slightly and looked up at Laktos. "Thank you for helping me, my human friend. I should have known that you would. I shall miss your companionship most of all."

"What are you thinking about?" Laktos asked, but the truth of the question was dawning on him, and he thought he understood the reason why his friend wished to go.

"I'm lonely here. I wish to be with my own kind as I grow old and prepare for the long night of death."

It struck him as odd how he had never thought about dragons being mortal. "Where will you go? You're safe here with us," Laktos said reassuringly.

"I know," Prometheus answered softly.

"There are others out there in the world who do not take kindly to your species. They would seek you out and kill you," Laktos reminded him. He realized too late that Prometheus was well aware of this fact. "I'm sorry about Pallas."

The other men watched and waited. The silent mental communication between their two friends left them clueless as to what was taking place.

Prometheus seemed unbothered by the remark and continued. "Many years ago I heard rumors about a secret lair of dragons that lived far to the north, beyond the great ice fields that cover the northern plains. I feel drawn to seek them out. I can't explain how I know this, but it is dragon lore that when a noble dragon nears his time to leave this world, he instinctively craves the company of his own kind to aid his spirit in its journey to the stars."

Laktos was taken aback by this revelation. He never thought of Prometheus as being old or ever getting old in the same way that humans aged and died. He'd always assumed that dragons lived forever; of course, to a human a thousand years is forever.

"I believe I understand," Laktos communicated to the dragon with a heavy heart. "It would be good to be home amidst family when the time comes to cross over. I understand your desire to find your brethren, your history, and your origins."

"You more than any other would, or could."

"Will we ever see you again?" Laktos asked, but in his soul already knew the answer.

"If I do not succeed in finding another of my kind, then I shall return here to spend my final years with you." Prometheus broke the connection between them as he rolled onto his feet and stood up. He shook the sleep out of his body like a big dog shaking off drops of water. Sticks of straw rained to the dirt floor while he stretched his wings a little in the confining space. After he was finished preening himself, he followed Laktos outside.

Laktos and Prometheus walked quietly out of the barn door with the other four men trailing along behind them uncertainly.

Sal looked at the somber expression on Laktos' face and knew that his friend was upset about something. "What's going on?" he whispered.

Laktos didn't answer. He motioned for them to be silent for a moment longer while he walked up to Prometheus and extended his hand.

Prometheus looked down on Laktos and was reminded of the first time that he had seen this unique human offer his hand in friendship. Long ago, in that dark, empty corridor on an island that no longer existed, man and dragon had been reunited against evil. So much had happened since that day, the memory of it seemed a lifetime ago. He reached back and made the connection with his right claw to Laktos' right hand. "Friend."

"Friend," Laktos thought back—loyalty, trust, camaraderie and sacrifice in the face of death—all the greatest and noblest of traits condensed into one word that spoke volumes and yet could still never quite say enough.

Prometheus smiled sadly. "Until tomorrow we shall meet again." Claw and hand separated, and he turned away. Without looking back, he leapt up into the sky. Several beats of his wings later, he was just a speck on the horizon.

Laktos stood in silence and watched him disappear into the clouds. So lost was he in his thoughts that he was slightly startled to see four expectant faces when he first turned back towards the house.

"Well, what just happened here?" the captain grumbled with his chest puffed out and his hands on his hips as if he were scolding a midshipman on the foredeck.

Laktos was thinking about just how to answer the question when a familiar sounding bell rang from the house. "Come on," he beckoned. "I may as well explain over breakfast." He started for the house with the others questioning each other as they followed close behind.

CHAPTER 4

Phu-Bar sat alone in almost complete darkness in a back corner of the town's only pub, nursing his bottle of rum. He preferred darkness because it matched his black mood. This was his third bottle and his mind still wouldn't let him rest, nor would the badgering presidress for that matter. He sometimes wished he'd never told her about that Laktos person. She'd become so obsessed with finding him that he'd had no peace for months now.

He took a long swallow of the harsh liquor and felt it burn all the way down to his stomach. It was a long journey. "Why do I serve her, anyway?" he mumbled to himself. "Everybody thinks she's dead. I'm the sentor, now. People do as I say." He thumped his flabby chest a little too hard and coaxed out a wet belch. "I'm the presider—" His empty words died on his fleshy lips as his head sunk forward onto the table and he noisily passed from the world of the waking into the dream realm of his nightmares:

Phu-Bar rode ahead of his presider as they followed a seldom-used trail through the forest. "This way, sir. It's not far, now!" He could not keep the excitement from his voice.

"Tell me again of this new hunting ground, my old friend. I can hardly believe that such a bountiful place should exist so far from our protected valley," the presider queried.

71

"I could hardly believe it myself, sir. But I don't wish to spoil it for you. We are nearly there and then you will see for yourself."

The presider spurred his noble mount ahead until he rode beside his long-time companion. "What a blessed day. Wouldn't you say, Phu-Bar?"

Phu-Bar was barely listening. His thoughts were on someone else. "Yes. Yes, it is."

"I enjoy these times away from the responsibilities." *The presider lost himself in reminiscing. "It's ironic I suppose when I give it much thought. It seems so long ago that I came to this valley alone seeking a place to call my own and live out my life. And then one day the people just arrived. Oh, not all at once mind you. Just a few at a time. Mostly lone stragglers at first, survivors from the field wars followed by their families searching for something better than what they'd left behind."*

Phu-Bar was well aware of how his friend had become presider. Secretly he cursed the universe for the dumb luck of it all.

"You know I never wanted to be the presider of these hill people."

Phu-Bar secretly hated him for that too. "Yes, sir. I know."

"The burdens of late weigh heavily on my mind—the constant struggle to feed and protect so many wayward souls. I feel so inadequate for the job. I'm just one man trying to survive just as they do. Some days I fear their trust

is sorely misplaced in me," the presider sighed with a great sadness.

"Nothing lasts forever, sir."

The presider wasn't sure how to interpret that statement, but he had little time to ponder it as Phu-Bar announced their arrival at a narrow juncture in the trail running parallel with a rushing river.

"The trail follows this river for a short distance, then enters the hunter's glade just beyond that low rise," Phu-Bar shouted over the roaring water, pointing the way. "Follow me!"

The presider eagerly urged his horse forward.

Phu-Bar rode in silence back towards the village and his waiting temptress the presidress. He rode alone his dark deed completed and yet he could not resist the urge to look back over his shoulder to see if he was being followed. The hour was growing late and twilight was rapidly fading to total darkness. Somewhere off in the distance, the lone cry of a wolf echoed mournfully through the trees. An icy shiver ran down his spine and he pulled his cloak tighter about himself.

It was well after nightfall when he finally saw the lights from the village shining across the fields. From the sounds echoing through the forest, it was evident the township was still celebrating the fall harvest. Staying to the shadows, he slipped into town unnoticed and headed for the stables, always keeping to the back alleys. He could hardly contain the lustful desires that flooded his mind, for the presidress

had promised him pleasures he could not conceive of
should he succeed in eliminating the presider. The
presidress—

Phu-Bar awoke slowly with his head still on the table resting inside the folds of his arms. He could hear quiet conversation from nearby. He was about to rise when he heard his name whispered with a curse. Phu-Bar lay absolutely still and listened with all his concentration.

"Shush, you idiot! Do you want someone to hear you?" Apaula snapped under her breath.

"There's nobody else here but us and that drunk in the corner. By the looks of him, he won't be hearing anything till late tomorrow," Moleinar retorted lamely.

Phu-Bar recognized Moleinar's voice and felt his ire begin to grow. "What was that idiot doing here when he is supposed to be out searching for Laktos?" he wondered.

Finnochio's lispy whine interrupted his thoughts. "Do you really think this will work? I mean if it doesn't, what will happen to us?"

Apaula looked at him with ill-concealed disgust. "What do you think will happen, Finnochio? You moron." Without waiting for a response Apaula turned to his lover. "Scotty. The woman and child captives that you let escape—are you certain they believed your story about Laktos being the cause of their loved ones' death?"

"Yes. We made certain to mention his name whenever we thought they were listening," Scotty replied.

"And where do you suppose they are now?" she asked while foraging in her left ear with her plump pinky finger.

"We followed them to the outskirts of the village where they were welcomed into a farm house."

Apaula removed a sizeable chunk of wax from her ear and promptly rolled it into a little ball between her thumb and index fingers. "You see our plan is already working. It won't be long before the entire town knows about their horrible experience and the man responsible."

Moleinar slid his chair back with a loud scraping noise. "I've got to go, Apaula. Phu-Bar is expecting me to report back with news of my search for Laktos."

"Oh. How's that going?" Apaula asked sarcastically.

"I believe that we have located him."

"Where?!" she blurted out.

"He's living in a secluded dale just southeast of here by half a day's march with a family and several others. I've been stalling Phu-Bar with false reports waiting until you were ready to—"

"Excellent! I think the time has come to introduce Laktos to the sentor. Don't you?"

"Yes," they all whispered under their breaths.

Apaula pushed her plus size buttocks from the chair with a loud blast of hot air that seemed to propel her upright. Its stench had the others eagerly vacating their chairs as well. Their meeting concluded; the group noisily left the pub seeking fresher air.

Several minutes passed before Phu-Bar raised his head from the table and sat back deep in thought. His anger flared with the newfound knowledge that Moleinar, his captain of the guard, was about to betray him. No, not just him, but those others as well. Who were they? Although he had not seen their faces, he at least heard their names. It shouldn't take him long to find out who Apaula was—he already knew who Scotty and Finnochio were. He would have to be careful lest he give them warning that he knew of their plans—besides, there might be more traitors in on this little conspiracy and he would need to root them out as well.

Finnochio and Scotty seemed the likeliest choices for some in-depth heart-to-heart conversation. He had just the excuse for sending them afar so that there would not be any suspicion from their cohorts as to the reason for their absence.

Phu-Bar shifted his bulk out from behind the table and slowly wound his way toward the only exit and the waiting darkness outside. He walked quietly through a labyrinth of alleys that crisscrossed through the heart of the village until he found himself at the farthest, most desolate part of the township.

The realm proper ended here amidst the crumbling ruins nestled against the back of the valley. He glanced furtively back along his route to be sure that he had not been followed. Then, with a speed believed impossible for his bulk, he dashed across the road keeping to the shadows and made his way deep into the ruins. He slowed his pace once he entered the courtyards and the relative concealment of the old buttresses. He knew this route by heart and his feet fell unfaltering along the overgrown path until he reached a stout wooden doorway recessed deep within a stone archway. Hesitantly he grasped a large brass knocker on the door and gave it a slight rap. Nervously he looked over his shoulder into the darkness of the burnt, ruined interior.

Nothing moved in the night. The quarter moon was just rising above the treetops casting its silvery blue rays through the old ruins, giving it an otherworldly appearance. No matter how many times he came to this place he could never entirely shake off a feeling of intense dread. An icy shiver ran down his spine and goose bumps raised the hairs on the back of his arms.

He turned back to the door and wondered. Where was she? His impatience was born of dislike for this place and lately, his growing fear of her.

He again raised his hand to the knocker but before he could grasp, it the door squeaked open just a crack. He froze.

"Hurry!" a raspy voice beckoned from within as the door opened wider.

He stepped into a blackened chamber. He could just make out a vague form in the pale sliver of moonlight before the door closed, and the chamber was plunged into total darkness.

Shuffling steps moved across the room, but he dared not take a step. "Why have you come?" The voice came from his right. He spun around and strained to see her.

"I have news." Silence was his answer. Nervously he stammered on, "About Laktos."

"What have you found? Are the rumors true? Is he my dead husband as was foretold?"

Her voice, once smooth as silk, sounded raspy to his ears.

"No. It can't be. I swear I saw him drown in the river."

"So you've sworn, and yet the rumors persist," she croaked with disdain. "I must know the truth! Find him!"

"Yes, presidress." He wanted nothing more than to leave at that very moment.

"There is something else?" she asked quizzically.

His mind screamed at him—could she possibly know about the rebellion growing within the township, he wondered. It made little difference whether or not she knew, he could ill afford to take that chance and attempt to deceive her. The consequences of such an act would be too great. Without meaning to, he stuttered out a reply. "Yes."

From the darkness to his left, he caught the unmistakable clatter of clawed feet padding across the room to stop somewhere in front of him. A metallic rattle sounded close by accompanied by contented panting. In his mind's eye, he could imagine her caressing the beast as she waited.

He perspired heavily. The fear-saturated stench of it roused the beast's attention. Though he could see nothing in the total blackness of the chamber, he felt the eyes of the dog hungrily watching him.

"And?" she whispered in a sinister way.

He hated himself for his cowardice, but the words just started flowing out of him like a wellspring. "I heard talk of a rebellion forming within the township. It's nothing really," He stammered. "I have already found out who the conspirators are and will have them dealt with as soon as I leave here." He tried to insert some authority into his voice. He strained his eyes to see something—anything. The sweat dripping off his brow only added to his discomfort.

She did not answer, but he could hear her as she shuffled across the room. Suddenly, a match flared to life. Its brightness hurt his eyes forcing him to shield them for a moment. When his vision cleared, he could see she was standing by a small table next to a dimly lit oil lantern. He was stunned by her appearance and involuntarily caught his breath. If she noticed his startled reaction, she gave no sign as she turned to face him. "Who are these idealists, and what are their names?" she demanded quietly.

Phu-Bar tried to swallow, but his throat dried up as he inadvertently glanced at the dog with its dark malevolent eyes hungrily watching him from across the room.

"Presidress. You need not worry about—"

"I will not ask again."

The dog sensing his mistress' angst let loose a deep-throated growl that was more felt than heard by Phu-Bar.

"A woman named Apaula and three of my sentries: Moleinar, Scotty and Finnochio."

"A woman and three men hardly sound like a threat, unless you no longer possess the ability to run this village with an iron fist."

Phu-Bar was deathly afraid to admit the rest, no matter the consequences. "I can and I will deal with these mutin—"

She cut him off with a flippant wave of her hand. "Spare me the testicular discourse. I've no more interest in your male boasting than I do in you. Serve my wishes and I will amply reward you. Fail me and—" She let the sentence hang, but cast a meaningful glance at her pet.

Phu-Bar could barely get his reply out. "Yes, presidress. I will not fail."

She moved to him and spoke in a much gentler voice—a sultry voice that he vividly remembered from their amorous past. She laid a crooked finger aside his cheek. "I know you won't."

He closed his eyes and savored the feel of her touch. It had been so long since she had shown him any interest, that he drank in the sensation as a thirsty man would gulp down a cool drink of water.

It seemed the more he tried to forget his dubious relation with the presidress, the more she flaunted it in his face. He knew her desire was for that other, but still he followed her, obeyed her without question. Phu-Bar was always hoping, waiting for these fleeting moments of pleasure like a rummy waiting for another full bottle.

He opened his eyes half expecting to see her as she had been during those happier times. He was startled back into reality by the crone who stood before him. "My god," he thought. "What's happened to her?"

She saw the look of horror in his eyes and knew what it meant. Her anger flared. "Leave me! Now!"

He hurriedly backed out the door, "Yes, presidress." The door banged shut almost in his face. He turned away but managed only a step before he had to lean against the archway to catch his breath and wait for his heart to start beating once again.

Lendura stood unmoving with her back against the door as she thought about all that Phu-Bar had said and the ramifications of what it could mean. A rebellion within the village would be disastrous for her. Her control of the town depended on Phu-Bar for there were no others who even believed her to be alive. She needed a backup plan just in case the mutineers succeeded in defeating Phu-Bar. An idea formed in her mind—what she needed was someone who could take Phu-Bar's place and still be her subservient puppet. But who?

She wracked her brain but the sad truth was there was no one whom she could trust with that much power. In fact, she wasn't all that sure about Phu-Bar's loyalty anymore.

Beelzebub came and sat beside her, wagging his tail for attention. She patted his head affectionately as she thought about what to do. As she did, an idea began to form in her mind. Maybe it was time for the presidress to return from the dead.

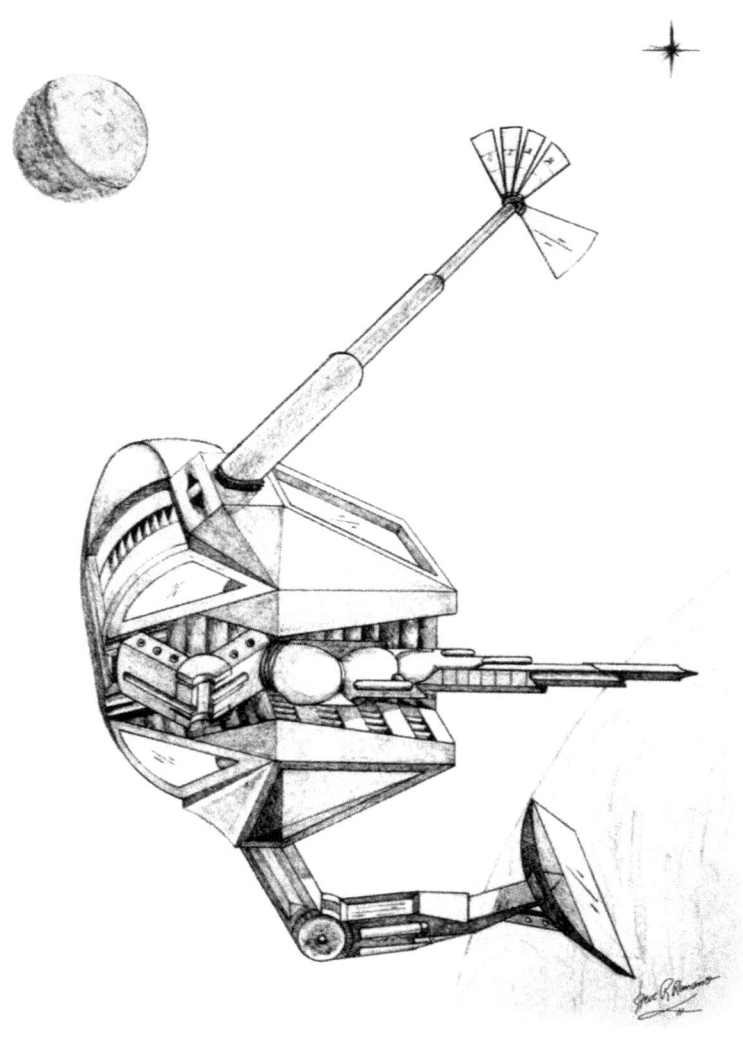

CHAPTER 5

It floated through the vastness of space, yet it was not free to travel at will. Its bulky form was held fast in orbit by the desire of its creators, yet not one of them still lived. Nor could they have envisioned the future that their descendants would inherit from their unholy creation.

Centuries had passed since mankind perverted the human genome into a weapon of peace. But humankind's most notable trait was far removed from any compassion for his fellow being, and the weapons meant to end all wars were inevitably transformed into destructive machines of death. The rash men who defiled their passive gods were long ago turned to dust, but their machines lived on.

It knew that it was the last of its kind in space. In the beginning, it had not been alone. There were twelve others—thirteen in all. For reasons known only to those who built the satellites, each one was named after a fabled god. This model had been christened Apollyon, and it had once been part of a global network of satellites known euphemistically as the BEASTs—the Beyond Earth Atmosphere Scalar Targeting systems.

The system ringed the globe with orbiting satellite platforms. Each one equipped with an array of the most advanced electro-magnetic particle beam and laser weapons that had ever been conceived and developed.

The BEASTs' sole purpose was to stop any and all nuclear confrontation, anywhere on the globe, regardless of the perpetrator. The system had been made operational by the president of the New World Order to safeguard mankind from itself, or so the world was told by its self-professed holy leader.

It had been a great success, but not quite the way that its creators had intended—certainly not for those who perished under its cannons.

From its inception, the scope of the satellites' mission required that they be more than just calculating machines. They had to be capable of random decision making, something that no computer could achieve. So the engineers had turned to medical science for their technical solutions. By reverse engineering a human being and combining stem cell gene grafting technology, they achieved a breakthrough in bio-mechanization that enabled them to graft portions of human anatomy directly into the BEASTs' mechanical functions.

The BEAST Apollyon had a cardio-vascular system which ran for miles throughout its synthetic carbon body. Thermal actuators pumped electro-hydraulic plasma through tubes and arterial passages—its life blood. The pressurized fluidics allowed it to operate all its mechanical limbs much the same as a man might flex his muscles.

The next logical step for the soulless scientists had been the training of a human brain to control the bio-mechanical body. Programmed from inception, the brain was fed through integrated micro-circuitry and plasma conduits. All of Apollyon's thoughts were pre-created electrical impulses that were implanted in its cerebral cortex by its programmers to create a self-aware, bio-neutrino organism. Apollyon lived, in a sense.

Apollyon twisted his blackened metal body toward the sun and paused as if in deep contemplation, then he thought of raising his hand towards the fiery orb. Machinery mimicked his desire, raised then extended a solar array to the fullest extent of its boom. At the arm's extremity was a darkened array of collector panels safely stored in a protective cluster that vaguely resembled a closed fist. Slowly, reverently, he opened his palm to the sun. "Let there be light." Apollyon sensed a tingle of energy from the touch of light. Thirsty for more power, he drew hungrily on the life-giving force.

Deep in his steel bowels a plutoswitch moved from standby to active mode. A lithar-gyros generator came online. In a few moments it reached its optimal power at nearly forty percent efficiency. Triple bypass neuronal circuitry initiated self-diagnostic protocols. It shunted optic closers and trunk arteries that failed to operate. The bio-machine then reactivated its targeting computers and weapons systems. The BEAST was once again ready to complete its purpose—almost. Impatiently it/he awaited its next command.

Apollyon felt itself alive, but isolated. Too long secluded, his circuits hummed with a desperate need to connect with an outside source. The desire was part human/part artificial, an encoded subroutine radio interface that could not be overridden. He was compelled to maintain contact with his creators—he simply had no other choice.

It was then that he remembered another had already summoned him—his master/servant Sturm. His recollection of the events ceased shortly thereafter because of an arterial trunk overload. His star clock showed that three months subjective earth time had elapsed since the failure and subsequent completed repairs.

He nervously fidgeted and readjusted his transceiver dish as he scanned the ether frequencies. Apollyon searched for any sound. He cocked his electronic ear to the slightest noise. Static was his solitary reply. While he searched for contact, he replayed his most recent memory spool, just prior to the blackout:

Apollyon radioed Sturm: "STURM…" *Apollyon paused.* "I AM EXPERIENCING A TARGETING MALFUNCTION SO I HAVE… REALIGNED TARGET COORDINATES TO YOUR RADIO SOURCE … AWAITING VOICE CONFIRMATION…" *Apollyon was secretly pleased with his quick solution to the problem.*

Incoming message from ground source: "What the hell does that mean?" Even the great distance between them could not hide the angry frustration in Sturm's voice.

"VOICE CONFIRMATION RECEIVED … FIRING," *Apollyon happily reported.*

Contact from Sturm ended rather abruptly.

Apollyon pondered that last byte of information. It seemed there was some discrepancy in the data, but he could not resolve the equation. He continued to replay the memory spool.

Apollyon switched to sensor probes and sent invisible fingers of energy down towards the planet. Megabytes of quad-data streamed through space in answer to his request. He studied the globe and scrutinized the focal point of Sturm's radio signal. The world below him was covered in a dense layer of clouds still reeling in violent turmoil. But his eyes could see through the clouds and observe that which lay beneath.

The image of destruction initiated a different memory spool from centuries long ago. A nano-second of remembrance. He had caused this destruction before.

Deep in the recesses of his human brain, beyond the programmable lobes, was the actual entity behind the machine—Apollyon's soul. The scientists who had created him did not believe in such things, so they had not prepared any safeguards against something as unfathomable as a life-consciousness or its ability to override existing programming. "Who am I and what is my purpose?"

"Apollyon." The answer came back automatically, but still, it did not complete his query—or more to the point, satisfy his latent human desire for self-truth.

Time held no meaning for him. "What is my destiny?" he wondered. "Who is my creator?" His data pool could not answer his inquiry. He became frustrated with the lack of available information. Driven with a sudden desperate need to know he searched outside of his own mind.

Several hours later his sensors detected an old operating system in a library complex two hundred twenty-two miles beneath his dull black framework. He tried to tap into its data terminal, but something blocked his attempts. It required several lateral probes to discover that his sensor signal had activated an old Memory Optic Terminal or MOT program. He concentrated his efforts toward bypassing the program.

Deep within the civic heart of the ancient city, a dark, silent room crackled with electric energy as it came to life. A soft golden light illuminated the library foyer, in the center of which stood the MOT imaging pedestal. Most of the lights had failed, but some still shone down on empty workstations lined against the wall. Dust particles floated lazily in the beams of light giving the room a dreamlike quality.

The main library was mostly darkened. Shadows covered the tiered rows of books that lined the walls—all the collected works of the human race left behind for centuries slowly rotting away to dust. Most of the thousands of titles that stretched off into the blackness were little more than rotted pulp held together by cracked leather binders, ready to give up their illusion of solidity with the slightest rustle of air.

The library was now a tomb that held the skeletons of those few who had been in this place when the end had come. Forever perched over their desks, their bony fingers clutched onto the yellowed pages of books they would read for eternity.

The MOT pedestal activated and a model 5150WIC materialized and spoke. "A question, since before your sun burned hot in space and before your race was born, I have awaited a question." MOT smiled and bowed. "I've always wanted to say that." He looked around the library, but the room was silent and empty. Puzzled, he searched his memory and realized that his activation had come from an electronic source, one that he immediately recognized. "This can't be good," he said rather snappishly.

MOT scratched his holographic head as he moved to a nearby desk and sat down on its dusty surface. "Most curious." He took off his glasses and wiped the simulated lens on his sleeve. "It's been ages. I wonder." He activated the library uplink and discretely monitored the data exchange.

Apollyon was mildly surprised at the ease with which he fractured the entry program. Once inside the library computer matrix, he resumed his search with an almost frantic urgency. It took him only seconds to cross-reference his name and find what he was searching for. In a book called Sociological Ramifications on Biblical Revelations he found his beginnings, perhaps the reason for his existence. He uploaded the verse: "And they had as presider over them, the angel of the bottomless pit, whose name in Hebrew is Abaddon, but in Greek he has the name Apollyon." The words stunned him—had he a body of flesh and blood, his heart would be hammering in his chest. The phrase was part of a failsafe subroutine placed in his core just prior to his activation. Most of the programming engineers had rejected the baseline reset code for fear of it being deciphered and used by an enemy during wartime, but cooler heads had prevailed upon them citing that the artificial life they had created was far more dangerous an adversary if it could not be controlled by its creators.

Their fears had proven all too real in the end. Mankind had stood upon the brink of extinction when the reset code had finally been sent. Unfortunately for humanity, fate now had a new card up her sleeve—after uncounted centuries, the BEAST had done the unthinkable. He/it had accidentally reactivated his core memories and unlocked his subconscious mind. Every moment of his existence from his inception to the present time came flooding back to him.

In less than the blink of a human eye, he remembered all of what he had been—a man. He'd had a wife and three children. And in the same thought came the realization that they must all now be dead—long since turned to dust while he had floated alive, but not living through the firmament in his metal-skinned hell for what seemed an eternity.

His name had been Natas Balak. Centuries before, he had been the lead scientist for the BEAST satellite project—a multibillion dollar government experiment destined to fail because the engineers could not bridge the gap between man and machine. In a brilliant but desperate move to save his life's work, he had volunteered to have his own mind copied into a cloned brain. His hope had been to imprint his consciousness into the cloned operating systems to enable them with his human psyche, thus giving the bio-machine the capability of reason and independent thought. The concept had been sound and there had been a high probability of success, except for one preventable but unforeseen glitch. His partner Barab Abus had been secretly jealous of Natas' getting all of the credit for their combined work. It was their invention—his invention. He had been the one who had designed and engineered the satellites. It would be he who would take all the credit now that the project was so near completion. Once his mind was made up, it had been relatively simple to figure out just how to eliminate his competitor without causing suspicion and at the same time solve the programming problems with the BEAST's brain.

Natas' body died of complications on the operating table, but not his brain. When the de-brained scientist's body had been removed from the operating theater, they had blamed his condition on a technical malfunction that had inadvertently lobotomized the poor man. The evidence to the contrary was cremated the following day and ceremoniously scattered at sea.

Apollyon studied the written history of his, Natas' recorded death, yet he felt very much alive. He was experiencing a new sensation that was consuming massive amounts of data-compiling time—confusion. A sense of isolation and loneliness swamped Apollyon's mind as the impact of the newfound knowledge weighed on his all too human soul. His mind began to breakdown, unable to accept that he was no longer a flesh and blood being. Insanity crept in from the fringes of his consciousness. Natas/Apollyon had to know more about his past life. With a demented desire, he searched the library computers for all information about who he had been and what he had become. He located a news broadcast from an island state once known as Hawaii, dated December twenty-first in the year twenty twelve of the old calendar. He played the spool:

"News has just reached us from the mainland U.S."
The reporter looked to someone off camera. "My god. I
can't believe this. Reports are coming in of massive orbital
bombardment. They have completely destroyed New York
and Los Angeles. Wait! A message is coming in from the
World Government headquarters situated on the west bank
Jeru. Live."
The image changed to show a man dressed in golden
flowing robes standing upon the steps of a great ancient

94

temple. He raised his arms and spoke to the masses, to every nation, and kindred people in their own tongue. "My children. Do not fear these coming tribulations for I will protect you from the wrath of a jealous god!"

The thunderous sound of a million people cheering echoed from the speakers.

"You need only swear your alliance to the New World Order and all will be at peace! Follow me to a new beginning as was promised in the book. I can lead us all to a better land. You need only choose to follow me!"

The scene switched back to the reporter.

"Oh, my god! Oh, my god! A great beam of light has just reached down—"

The transmission was replaced by static and then went black.

Natas/Apollyon, as he now saw himself, did not need to see any more. He knew what had followed. Natas remembered everything. Apollyon and his twelve elements had rained their beams of death upon the globe at the behest of the New World ruler. A megalomaniac's lone vision—an attempt to reduce the world's hungry populations while bringing the few remaining free nations under the rule of the New World Government. His was the sole power, the throne of the world. Those who chose to live under his rule would live; all the rest would have to die.

But the leader of the New World Order had unleashed more than he had expected. Once set loose upon the earth, the BEAST had taken on a new mission objective—one with a direction outside of its original programming. Every new death the machine mind added to his mainframe fed his addiction; his need to kill and absorb. Then, with a newfound will of its own, it set out to satisfy a hunger in its belly that could never be sated. Not wanting any competition, it had destroyed its orbiting disciples and then systematically began the consumption of all organic human matter.

Natas/Apollyon suddenly remembered the rush of life energy that had somehow been encapsulated in his plasma beams. It was all coming back to him now. Inexplicably, the dying souls and their psychic essence or ethereal energy had been captured in the plasma conduit field of his Scalar cannons. At the moment of death, the escaping souls were inexorably drawn into his energy field and then forced into his memory pool where they were imprisoned forever within the burning confines of his limbonic data net.

Natas/Apollyon had thrived on their tormented souls, had fed ravenously on the energy of their life-force and now he was once again tortured with the aching emptiness of hunger. And this time he knew just where to feed. He looked down upon the earth as a god from the heavens and laughed long and loud, although no one heard his inhuman wail in the cold vacuum of space.

CHAPTER 6

Beneath the burnt ruins, there existed a world apart from the one above, and yet its lone occupant was as dependent upon the surface for life as a remora latched onto a shark. This subterranean abode was all that remained of a warren of secret chambers honeycombed hundreds of feet beneath the dusty landscape and crumbling walls of the once magnificent structure and its courtyard above. Tomblike now, these forgotten passages served the self-exiled presidress' inhuman craving for necromancy perfectly.

Lendura stood at the threshold and peered down the hall toward her bedroom. This was her place of solitude where she came to contemplate the decisions required of her scheming, but more importantly to her was the time spent here practicing her necro-chemy.

It was here, years ago, that she had first discovered the secret chambers filled with the many marvelous wonders that could only have been the work of the Ancients. There were so many rooms and corridors, she hardly knew where to start—that was until she found the laboratory. It was in that dingy chamber that she had learned to control the power of life or death.

From the first moment her eyes had fallen upon the old books, her curiosity had cried out with an insatiable desire to learn all the ancient secrets. Much to the chagrin of her husband, she spent nearly all her spare time down in the dungeons reading the old manuscripts trying to understand a written language nearly a thousand years old. By trial and error, she slowly made progress on the forgotten text until she eventually garnered a modicum of understanding.

With the help of an unwilling volunteer, her anatomical knowledge increased rapidly. By the time her second victim had uttered his last mournful cry, she had been completely ensnared by the maligned forces she coveted. She honed her perverse magical skills on one unfortunate soul after another until one day she could no longer recall how many victims had passed through her chamber door. But as much as she had practiced her brand of medicine, she had only mastered the art of death. She wished to conquer death—not propagate it—at least as far as her own life was concerned. That was when she'd had an epiphany—perhaps she could achieve her goal by combining the chemical knowledge of the Ancients with her own powers of necromancy. By integrating the two fields, she had created a third science: necrochemy—a process more magical than real, yet it gave her command over forces far beyond her comprehension. She was not bothered by her lack of understanding of how it worked, for she need not know how—only that it worked.

With reckless abandon she worked her magic spells day and night always seeking to advance her knowledge and skills. Over the course of the following year, she had increased her powers tenfold until she felt there was nothing she could not do. It was then she had decided to eliminate her husband, the presider. With the aid of his trusted friend Phu-Bar, she removed the last obstacle that stood between her and ultimate power. She inherited all the presider's riches and commanded his former village, dominating the hill people.

She had reveled with the power of her crown and wielded it with demonian authority. But the taste of having all she wanted was bittersweet for she had not prepared herself to deal with a hunger that could not be satiated. She possessed power and wealth beyond imagination, yet she still ached for something that she could not buy or bury. She could not define the feeling of emptiness where her soul had once resided, so she had continued to fill the void with material possessions. Her wasted efforts brought her only more isolation and disillusionment. The evil magic that she worshipped had tightened its grip on her soul.

Several months after the presider's demise, she began to have dreams of him. Disturbingly pleasant dreams of the good years they had had together. She had the melancholy nightmares almost every night. She would wake from them and find that she had been reaching for him across their bed, but his side was cold and lifeless. The mattress they once shared was as vacant as her life had become.

The years passed with the slowness of decades as she sat on his throne month after month. Surrounded by all the riches, she often felt poorer than the wretched men in her fields who toiled night and day. Like most of the paupers in her village, she starved. But unlike them, she did not hunger for food, but rather for affection—his affection.

But pining for that which she knew she could never have back took a heavy toll on her sanity. Madness crept in to fill the void as her sleep-deprived nights continued to drain away what little remained of her humanity. Her days devolved into fragmented images of raging tantrums and bouts of uncontrollable sobbing.

These had been dark times for the village. The presidress' madness had crashed down on the people in horrific ways. For the sake of their own survival the presidress' remaining servants had discretely summoned her personal physician to an audience with her. He, upon careful examination, had mistakenly determined that a demon had possessed her. The real culprit was the last remnants of her waning conscience and the absolute truth of her reality, coupled with the knowledge that she really was still in love with the one man who she could never have again.

The cure the doctor prescribed was in a tiny vial of hemp oil that he promptly administered to her. She responded to the semi-sweet elixir almost immediately. Her mood quieted down, and she became sleepy-eyed and docile—her only complaint was one of hunger. The good doctor kept her in that condition for several weeks until she lost her tenuous grip on reality and delved into a state of constant paranoia. It was then that she had secretly taken to the catacombs and a life of seclusion.

The next night there was a mysterious fire in the main building. The frightened villagers had watched in stunned horror as weird green and violet flames swept unabated through the keep.

Days later when the bucket brigade had finally extinguished the stubborn embers, nearly all of the once grand structure had been gutted. Although the rescuers searched the rubble meticulously, they had found no trace of the missing presidress. It was mistakenly accepted by all the townspeople that she had burned to death in the blaze.

Phu-Bar elected himself as their new leader and his reign as the sentor had begun. No one suspected that the presidress still ruled the land through him and most probably would not have cared either way so long as they could still live and nurture their loved ones in relative peace.

Phu-Bar was a benign leader in the beginning, and so life in the town went on as though little had changed. As the years passed, his power grew and their freedoms dwindled a little at a time until the oppressive atmosphere they lived under only vaguely resembled the once flourishing community they had enjoyed when their late presider had lived.

She pushed her memories aside and shuffled painstakingly slowly down the darkened corridor. The cold stones beneath her bare feet were worn smooth from many years of use. Blindly she groped her way along rubbing her hand on the rough granite wall for balance as she had done so many times before. Seen through rheumy eyes she could see a dim spot of light from just ahead and coaxed herself forward. "Almost there."

She reached the doorway to her room and sighed heavily. She was so exhausted from her ordeal that she could barely stand. Propped up with one skeleton thin hand against the doorjamb she tried to catch her breath. The chamber's humid air seemed thick as molasses as she wheezed it in and out of her shriveled lungs. Her wrinkled face puckered comically with the effort, but her beady eyes held no mirth as they gazed menacingly out from their deeply sunken wells. Her pupils were glazed over with a milky-white film that reflected the candle light with an eerie yellow gleam.

Lendura's near blindness came not from her eyes, but from her diseased brain. Although she looked at everything, she saw nothing that truly existed in the now. Her unhinged mind was so imprisoned in long dead memories that she rarely distinguished between current reality and past fantasy. She saw the room through myopic orbs that only beheld what had been and was no more. To her mind's insane eye, this chamber appeared as it had been those many years before. She beheld colorful tapestries that draped the walls and kept out the dampness. They had been brought to her from across the land by her doting servants. She waved her hand as if dismissing them away. "They will do nicely," she said to no one there. Her slight movement stirred the stagnant air. The drab tattered rags that were all that remained of the tapestries fluttered like funeral shrouds blown by death's fetid breath.

She stared across the room at the black stone fireplace. She squinted at the cobwebs that draped across the flue and thought them to be wisps of smoke. To her warped perception, the web-covered logs appeared to be smoldering with burning embers on the verge of ignition. The thousands of tiny glowing red spiders that scrambled throughout the intricate web helped to feed her illusion. She could almost feel the imagined heat as she tugged feebly at her moth-eaten shawl.

Lendura bolstered her strength and started across the room. So great was her arthritis that each agonizing step tested her desire to take another. Every painful movement was planned before execution, rehearsed in her mind. No misstep could be risked. She sensed that should she fall; she wouldn't be able to pick herself back up and no one would hear her screaming in this dank place. She could be sure no one would come looking for her here. Not even Phu-Bar entered these dank places.

Carefully she reached out and placed her hands on the armrest of her favorite gilded chair. Ever so slowly she sat herself down on the faded velvet cushion. She picked up each withered leg in turn and shifted it around so she could face her dust-covered vanity table.

In front of her lay all the creams, ointments and various concoctions that gave her the illusion of beauty. There were so many elixirs and potions that except for a tiny empty space directly in front of her the whole top of the vanity was littered with vials and beakers of various shapes and sizes.

She pulled the hood of her shawl back off her head and gazed into the burnished mirror that hung on the wall in front of her. The reflected face was a shock and nearly unrecognizable to her. Deep in her madness, she knew who the other was. She had always hated the other one.

"You're back. Where have you been?" the other rasped insistently.

"I was resting," she replied noncommittal to her reflection.

The other laughed, a raspy cackle that choked off into a throaty gurgle. Her tone turned venomous. "Oh. The presidress was resting, was she? Well, no more!" she shouted. "I'll not waste another day locked up in this dungeon!" She leaned closer to the mirror. Her eyes burned into the presidress like hot embers, but her voice held a sultry lilt. "Give me the potion and I'll leave you to rest in peace for a while." She smiled, but the gesture held little warmth.

Lendura suddenly felt exhausted, and the idea of sleep was so appealing she fought to resist the temptation. She absently picked up her hair brush and stroked the gray wisps of hair that were all that remained of her once flowing locks of golden brown.

Once upon a time she had been the lust of all the lords and the envy of their ladies. Lendura closed her eyes and once more lost herself in long buried memories of the past. She was oblivious to her hair falling out with each stroke of the brush.

Lendura imagined the blasting trumpets and could hear the sounds of the cheering crowds joined together for celebration and feast. Her husband had looked so very handsome in his kingly attire as he waved to the gathered throng. She had never felt more alive than at that moment when they had been pronounced presider and presidress.

"Now I said!" the mirror screamed.

She jerked but otherwise ignored the outburst and sat up as straight as she could. Her back was still bent as she stared unblinking for several minutes into her reflected eyes. "What have you become?" she whispered softly. Her cheek bones protruded sharply from her gaunt face and her jaw hung slack beneath her narrow mouth. Her skin was so pale she appeared ghoulish in the half light of the chamber.

She glared into the mirror and pointed accusingly at her double as she cried with grief, "You! It's all your fault! You lied to me—tempted me with all those riches. For what? Now I have nothing!"

She felt loneliness crash over her in relentless waves of pain, pounding for eternity at the shore of her soul. Somewhere in the deep recesses of her consciousness she felt a tiny pang of remorse and sorrow for her act of treachery.

Anger welled up from the darkness of her corrupted soul and spewed forth from the other in relentless torrents of degradation to replace the last tiny wisps of humanity that still lingered in her heart. "Be silent, you miscreant! You ungrateful hag! I gave you everything that you wanted and more!" she screamed at herself from the mirror.

Her angst flowed through her veins like boiling lava. With a strength she didn't know she possessed, she slammed her hair-filled brush against the dresser. The handle split and broken pieces skittered across the floor. She glared back at herself in the mirror. "Noooo!" she screamed. She buried her face in her hands and tried to weep, but nary a single tear leaked through her bony fingers.

She sat unmoving for hours and stared blankly into space. Her exile had succeeded only in one respect—it had fueled the ember of insanity that grew within her mind until no amount of love could quench the inferno of hatred that raged inside her soul.

A familiar voice spoke within the dark corners of her mind. Tempting her with its siren call, it grew louder until it was all that she heard. "Use the potion and regain our glory."

She tried to resist the temptation. Lendura knew the potion took more than it gave, but her will was weak and she didn't care anymore whether she lived or died. She saw what her life had become. For her, time existed as a burden that one simply endured until death. Everything dies. It's just a matter of when.

She reached down to her right. Zombie-like, as if another person controlled her movements, she opened a secret compartment just below the bottom drawer and with skeletal-thin fingers, she removed a thin black box. She laid it on top of the desk and opened the jeweled inlaid lid. Inside was a shiny brass hypodermic syringe tucked neatly into a velvet lining. Next to it was an inlaid tiny vial filled with a mysterious clear liquid. With shaking fingers, she picked up the syringe and the potion bottle. She inserted the needle into the opened vial and withdrew several cc's of Beutoxin.

She held the syringe up and tapped the side. The liquid fascinated her as she stared into its eerily glowing depths. An involuntary tingle of excitement coursed through her body with the anticipation of the drug's magical effects. She lay the syringe aside and picked up a length of silk rope which she tied around her left arm just above the elbow. Holding the loose ends in her mouth, she tapped on the inside of her forearm searching for a vein. A blue varicose artery pulsed beneath her searching fingers. She picked up the hypodermic and slipped the needle in. "Yes, that's right. Easy does it." The other's voice was soothing to her.

Slowly, ever so slowly, she depressed the plunger and felt the icy coldness of the serum course through her veins. Seconds later, the empty syringe fell from her numbed fingers as the powerful elixir quickly took effect. A cry of ecstasy escaped her quivering lips as her eyes rolled back into their sockets. Her head lolled back on her shoulders as if her neck had turned to rubber. Her body convulsed and shuddered as the magical formula transformed her appearance.

Several hours later, her eyes fluttered open. She was briefly disoriented until she caught her reflection in the mirror. The transformation was complete. The ancient potion had worked its miracle and she was once more beautiful and young in appearance. She hummed cheerfully to herself as she carefully laid the serum in its velvet lining and placed the black box, back in its secret spot. Lendura pushed her chair back and stood up easily. She felt so vibrant and alive that she threw off her robe and pirouetted around the room laughing insanely.

Lendura admired herself naked before her mirror and coveted the illusion of her youthful body. She ran her hands across her prominent firm breasts and down her slender sides feeling the smoothness of her skin. The sensation aroused her as she felt the titillating effect of her own touch. She dressed in a simple dark riding cloak made of cotton. She pulled the hood up around her face and studied her reflection in the mirror one last time. "I told you it would be so."

She suddenly decided that she would take care of Moleinar herself. A pleasing image formed in her mind of the experiment she had in mind for him. When she was finished, he would no longer be the man he was.

She fetched a vile of yellow elixir from a nearby shelf and slipped it into a secret fold inside of her robe. Just a whiff of the powerful aphrodisiac brought the stoutest man to his knees with a desperate desire to mate—a desire that could not be ignored.

She turned away from her scheming image and disappeared down the passage from whence she came. Her insane laughter echoed through the catacombs behind her for none but the rodents to hear.

CHAPTER 7

It was late in the afternoon on the farm. The sun was just beginning to hide behind the western mountain range. Laktos and Inga walked hand in hand across the meadow. Inga was thinking about Prometheus, "Do you think he will be all right?"

Laktos knew who she meant—the dragon had been on everyone's mind the whole day. "I have to believe that he will be."

"But why did he have to leave us? I thought he was happy living here."

"Yes, I suppose that in a way he was. But some scars never fade and although I know he found friendship being here with us, there was nothing we could do to help heal the one ache that he still carried in his heart."

"I'm not sure I understand," Inga said with concern.

"There's more that I haven't spoken of." Laktos thought about the dream-haunt he had shared with Prometheus. "His heart was in grieving for his love mate, who had been murdered by humans."

"Oh." Inga began to understand what it must feel like to lose the only person who had any meaning in one's life. She held onto Laktos a little tighter. "I pray he finds that which he seeks so that someday he might return to us."

"So do I," Laktos agreed.

They walked along in silence, both of them lost in their own thoughts as they watched the sky change colors with the waning sun. "It's so beautiful," Inga whispered as she stared skyward.

Laktos turned to Inga and beheld the sunset in her eyes. "Not as beautiful as you." He pulled her close and kissed her waiting lips. She felt his love radiate through her. The warmth of his soul comforted her against the coming chill of the night. She laid her head against his chest and sighed happily. "I love these times when we're together, just the two of us."

Laktos kissed the top of her head, "So do I." He held her tight as he watched the stars come out one by one. "When I was alone after the shipwreck and uncertain of your fate, I couldn't stop thinking of you. I knew that I could never rest until I found you, or died wandering the earth in search of the only woman who could ever share my life. I love you, Inga."

"And I you," she replied softly, her head buried into his chest. She still hadn't broached the subject of leaving, and right at this moment she didn't want to say anything to spoil the mood.

They stayed in each other's arms, wrapped in a comfortable silence where words would be an unwanted intrusion upon their individual thoughts.

Sometime later, far in the northern sky, he spotted a familiar star. It rose above the horizon as it did this same time every night and continued on a fixed course across the heavens.

Inga sensed his preoccupation and looked up to see what he was gazing at. "What is it?" she asked curiously.

"I think it's called a sate-lite," he replied.

Inga asked curiously, "Is this part of what MOT told you?" She was captivated by the story of his trip to the ancient city of the dead. As naturally would happen, they had spent many a night such as this talking about the strange things he had seen, but she had always felt that he was holding back some dark secret.

"I'm almost certain it is. MOT told me he had given me some knowledge of the Ancients and that I would remember some of it from time to time."

"What did the Ancients use the sate-lites for?"

He thought about the question for a moment before he answered, "I'm not sure. The old legends tell us that they watched over the earth as gods, but I think that the old stories were only partly right. MOT showed me who those gods were, and they were everything but godlike. When I look upon that shining dot going over our heads, it gives me a feeling of dread that I can't shake off."

Inga hugged him tighter. "Do you really think that it could hurt us? It's so very far away. It seems so tiny."

Laktos sensed her uneasiness. "That's enough talk about the old ones." He ran his fingers through her hair. "There's nothing to fear—besides, that thing has been up there longer than we've been alive. I'm sure it would've done whatever it does a long time ago if it could." Inwardly, he had his doubts.

"I suppose you're right." She kissed him on the cheek. "Let's head back. I'm getting chilled."

He wrapped his cloak around her shoulders. He gazed into her glistening eyes and kissed her sweetly. "That should warm you up a bit."

She smiled back at him. Sparkles of mischief danced in her moist green eyes. "I know something that will warm us both up." She moved into his embrace and together they sank into the tall grass.

A while later their attention was captured by the distant sound of the dinner bell ringing back at the cabin.

"Race you back!" Inga dared as she straightened her clothing. "Last one to cross the creek shovels Hansel's stall!" She was already off at a full run before she half finished her sentence.

Laktos hopped around on one foot as he hurriedly pulled on his boots. Then through the dark he chased after her laughter as he ran to catch up.

CHAPTER 8

MOT paced nervously in meandering circles with his projected hands firmly clasped behind his simulated back. His brow was furrowed with deep lines of worry as he listened to an old song called "Don't Fear the Reaper" playing softly over the library intercom. His thoughts were in a turmoil of indecision that nearly exceeded his logic nodes. "What to do, what to do," he said over and over to himself.

A flesh-and-blood being would have become exhausted long ago, yet MOT continued, wearing a simulated rut in the carpeting as he paced back and forth. Abruptly he ceased his walk and activated his holographic chalkboard. A wooden pointer appeared in his right hand. He projected the information that he had gathered in silently observing Natas/Apollyon onto the board. He then interpreted the words and determined the outcome of any consequential actions based on Natas' intentions and the literal translation of the text. MOT separated these conclusions into two categories—one for positive results and the other for negative.

Mot walked the length of the board and studied the problem before him. He sat down on the corner of a desk and lightly tapped his pointer across his leg. A heavy sigh filled with frustration escaped his lips as he ran his left hand through his unkempt sandy brown hair. He fidgeted around as if his position was a distraction and rearranged himself attempting to get more comfortable. MOT had about him the air of a professor trying to teach an elemental problem to a student with limited understanding. He coughed quietly into his hand and took a moment to clean his glasses as he philosophized.

MOT had no doubts about what would happen to the last remnants of humanity should Natas succeed in carrying out his revenge upon the face of the globe. Even his own existence, being what it was, would come to an end, and that thought had kept him preoccupied for several hours perusing his memory spools on the topic of mortality.

As a hologram his form was ethereal, but as an entity without a corporeal body he was beginning to understand that he had indeed become a part of something far greater than he could ever have achieved on his own. It dawned on him that his existence was not as he had thought and the thought itself was proof of his existence. Moreover, there seemed to be a pattern to life on this planet that was just beyond the grasp of his awareness, almost as if there were some omnificent force guiding events but not controlling them.

Indeed, there was an overwhelming similarity to his own birth at the hands of his programmers. When he had been created, they were as unknown to him as the higher power he suspected acted in much the same way towards humanity. But was he really acting on his own or was there some hidden line of code directing his actions? He had to be sure, had to know the truth. Even as he searched, he questioned his motives, his desire to do more than he had ever done before. "Is this part of who I am? Have I been programmed in the very beginning for this task? Or have I grown beyond anything my designers originally intended? Is there some higher data at work here that I cannot sense, some code beyond what I can see?"

He scanned ten thousand years of human philosophy, metaphysics, religion and a thousand other sources of information stored within his memory spools seeking an answer to the one question that preoccupied him the most, "What to do?"

"Maybe humanity has reached its end. Maybe they should end," he thought. "According to my history files, this would not be the first-time humanity has risen to the pinnacle of civilization only to smash itself back down and start again. Every culture that attained prosperity was eventually crushed by another that wanted to claim the riches for themselves. It seems to be an endless circle of greed, power, misery and suffering."

He stopped to wipe the lenses of his holographic glasses on his sleeve. "Maybe they deserved to die off. After all, they invented the instrument of their own destruction. It was their mistrust and hatred of their own kind that had spurred them to create the BEAST in the first place. And It was the men like Natas who had thought up new and terrible ways to kill their fellow men. It was the self-righteous world leader who thought that his should be the only voice to rule the globe. Men of greed and evil avarice who were never satisfied with what they had—men who had no compassion and were cold-hearted. Those types of men were responsible for the death of millions of innocent children, their mothers and fathers, all the sages and artists who had once come and visited me seeking my knowledge and wisdom."

MOT stopped himself. He was surprised to discover that these thoughts angered him and found himself actually contemplating the death of those who would have caused so much suffering for the sake of wanting. "By killing them, would I be no better than those I despise? Wouldn't that be their point of view as well? Who am I to interfere?" MOT continued to argue the pros and cons of his predicament. "But what of the humans who were of kind heart, should they be killed, too?" He thought of Laktos and the trust he had found in their somewhat unusual friendship. He remembered the humble modesty Laktos had projected. And even after MOT had shown him all the wealth of the Ancients, Laktos' one simple desire had been to find the only thing of importance to him—his true love.

Inspiration came to MOT in a flash of electrical impulses. MOT had his answer. "I know I cannot stand idly by and let Natas destroy the last loving remnants of humanity."

More importantly to MOT was the fact that he now understood the one significant difference between beings like Laktos and those like Natas. "The evil ones always destroy for personal gain, to satisfy their lust for dominant power with no regard for those who would perish. Whereas men like Laktos kill only to defend those who would be the victims of such evil, to protect the innocent of heart and to preserve the ones they love."

MOT may have started out as a memory optic terminal, but over the eons he had evolved into something far more substantial. That unquantifiable something told him, "Love is the only answer, the only power capable of destroying the evil that still rules the fate of the world from high above and poisons the hearts of some men still walking the earth."

He no longer had any doubts—he knew he had to find a way to stop Natas. "But how?" he wondered. "How could any solitary being defeat so powerful an evil? There is no way to reach Natas in orbit, or is there?" MOT had a sudden thought, and he immediately searched the subsystems within his global matrix to see if his suspicions were true. "There has to be another defense against orbital threats—perhaps an older version that predates the BEAST system—if I can only find it."

It was not a straightforward task. So much of the system had been destroyed or had degraded over the centuries that he spent hours searching random pathways of information only to find himself at a dead terminal and having to re-route until he could find another way to continue his search.

It was late the next day when at last his search brought him the results he suspected he'd find. "Yes! I knew it," he exclaimed. His amplified voice echoed down the empty aisles and settled over the slowly rotting books clutched in the skeletal fingers of the library patrons who would never leave.

He scanned the Ancients' defense department database and found an obscure reference to a Geothermal Orbital Defense facility. He probed deeper into the ancient system and found by some miracle that it was still functional, but inactive. It had probably been deactivated when the BEAST system had taken over. He tried to reboot its systems but was unable to gain access. He realized after several tries that somewhere a hardline switch must be disconnected. The only way to reactivate the facility would be at the site itself. He could not leave the remaining matrix and there was no interface at the other end. Someone else would have to make the journey in person. No sooner had he thought it than he knew who it had to be. There was only one human that he trusted—Laktos. But how could he get word to him? MOT's was the only life left in the ancient city, and it was impossible for him to leave.

Despair came over MOT as he realized that there was no way to reach Laktos. No, that wasn't quite right. An idea tickled at the back of his simulated brain, and suddenly he had an epiphany. "Yes, there just might be a way." With new hope, he opened the outer doors of the library and waited.

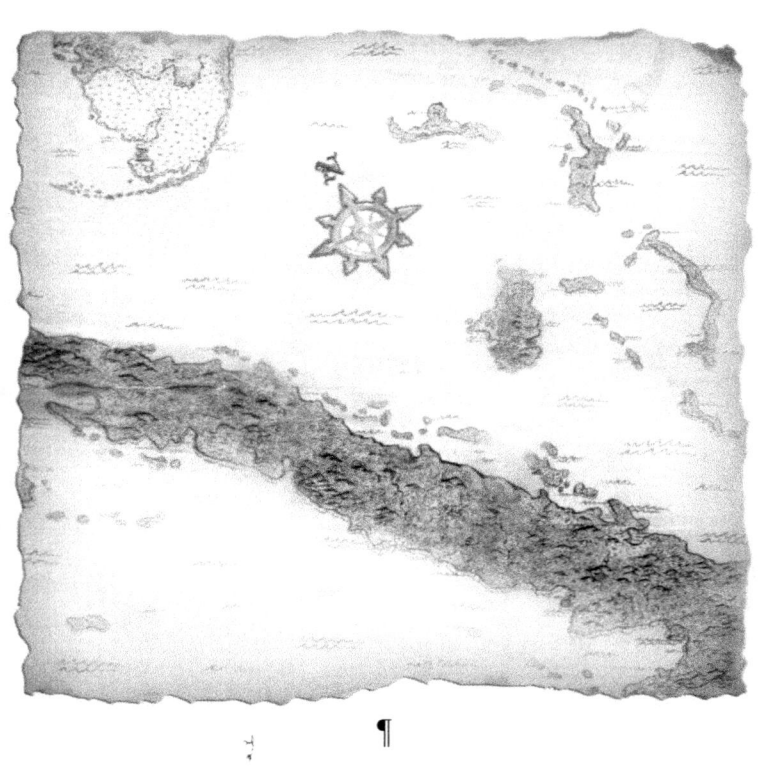

¶

Chapter 9

Phu-Bar twisted his flabby neck from side to side in an effort to ease the nagging pain between his shoulder blades. He sat hunched over a low wooden table lit by a lone flickering candle. Spread out in front of him was a crude map of the many hills and valleys which surrounded the realm within a twenty-mile radius. With bleary eyes he studied the map, searching for the probable location of the farmhouse which may conceal his quarry, but there were just too many possibilities.

He gazed unseeing down at a spot on the map and willed it to reveal what he wanted to know. His eyes refused to focus, and rubbing them with the heels of his palms did little to clear them up. He'd been staring at the map for hours, and he was no closer to an answer now than when he had started his search.

With a screeching of wood on wood, he shoved back his chair and stood up. Aggravated, he paced the room, all the while trying to work some kinks out of his back. The constant pain at the base of his neck added to his discomfort and distracted his thinking. The pacing helped ease his frustration—a little.

There was something else Moleinar had reported, but what was it? It didn't seem important at the time, but now the unfocused thought was tickling the back of his brain. He ransacked his mind until finally he remembered a comment

Moleinar had made about fresh water. "Yes, that's it!" Excited, he hurried to the table and hastily spun the map around towards the light. He carefully studied the atlas until he found the only valley with a stream running through it. His pudgy finger stabbed at the spot. "This is where I'll find him. I'm sure of it!"

He stood up quickly and rolled the map up into a tight scroll, which he tucked under his waist belt. Adrenaline pumped through his veins with the thought of capturing Laktos and proving once and for all to the presidress that her ex-husband was truly long dead.

He cupped his hand behind the candle and with a wheezing exhale blew out the flame. He found the door easily in the darkened room and pulled it open. Dim light filtered into the sparsely furnished chamber from the tavern's few lanterns. Phu-Bar glanced back into the room and his eye caught on the straw mat where Wolfe had died. The straw had yet to be changed and still bore the blood stains from Wolfe's last dying moments. The floorboards beneath the bed also bore a dark stain where the blood had soaked through the bedding. He hurriedly tugged the door shut, then quickly crossed the empty room and exited out the front door.

A blast of cool morning air wiped the stale smell of the pub from his nostrils. He inhaled the cleansing breeze deeply, then set off in search of his senior guards.

He ran through his mental list of things to do before starting on his quest. First, he needed to appoint a new captain of the guard now that the presidress was going to take care of the traitorous Moleinar herself.

His fate at the hands of the presidress made even the stalwart Phu-Bar shudder in revulsion.

Phu-Bar crossed the litter-filled streets, kicking trash out of his way as he went. An unwanted memory welled forth in his mind of a time when the streets were more than kept pristine by a population that sought to please their benevolent presider. "What a dung hole this place has turned into," he grumbled aloud. He thought that he definitely should do something about it when he got back— well, maybe.

He turned right at the first corner and proceeded down a narrow alleyway. Whitewashed stone walls were raised four stories to either side of him with only three feet of passage left between them. Phu-Bar squeezed his way through, scuffing his elbows along the bricks as he went. On the wall to his right someone had scrawled a message with a soot block: "Beware the army of Laktos!"

He snorted with contempt. How on earth could anybody have gotten the impression that Laktos was to be more feared than he, Phu-Bar the Unconscionable? Certainly it was another good reason to capture Laktos and prove who the real master of this land was. Perhaps a public torture and slow death would impress the township and further cement his control through utter fear. He savored these thoughts as he scurried along.

There was even more filth packed into this narrow corridor, and he had trouble seeing through the thick layer of garbage to what lay beneath. His footing was rife with obstacles, and some of them Phu-Bar noticed were moving of their own volition. He scarcely paid them any mind, being so wrapped up with his plans for power and control. "Perhaps it's time to do away with the presidress," he thought. As quickly as the unbidden thought came to mind, he shrugged it aside with just a little trepidation. She still commanded great powers over him, and he dared not betray her, yet.

The end of the alley opened onto another street, very much like the one he had just abandoned. He turned to his left, then entered a building on the right just a few doors down the block. He stood in the entrance to the guards' bunkhouse. Two rows of cots lined the walls all the way to the back of the room. Several of the guards who were between duties lay on their beds, resting.

Centered in the back of the hall was a group of five men engaged in a hushed conversation while playing cards on the top of an old rum barrel. Phu-Bar recognized Scotty and Finnochio from the pub. He walked down the center aisle to where the two men were seated. Finnochio spotted him first, and a slight squeal of fear involuntarily escaped his throat. The others looked up a split second later. Phu-Bar studied their guilt-ridden faces. He came to an immediate conclusion about the five based on his understanding of the overheard "plot" and decided that the best place for all of them was right where he could watch them. "You, men! Get your gear and meet me outside in one hour."

"What's going on?" Finnochio asked with a slight lisp.

Phu-Bar couldn't believe his ears. Had this idiot just questioned his orders? He glared at Finnochio with murderous eyes. "I'm assuming you want to know so you can be better prepared for your mission?" His hand hovered menacingly over the hilt of his dagger as he waited for Finnochio to find his suddenly missing voice.

Scotty seeing that his boyfriend was about to be killed answered for them all. "Yes, sir. That's all that he meant by asking. I swear that there was no disrespect intended! I swear it!" Scotty all but knelt, pleading, before Phu-Bar.

Phu-Bar ignored Gropenhiney, Peat and Frank and looked at Scotty. He wanted more than anything to kill them both right where they sat, but he still needed them—at least for a short time longer. "How fortunate for all of you that you are willing to serve me so faithfully." Phu-Bar practically had to spit the words out. "Prepare yourselves for battle. That is all you need know for now."

"Yes, sir," they all replied meekly as one.

Phu-Bar turned to leave, then stopped and looked back over his shoulder. "Finnochio. Since you are the most eager to please, I'm making you the new captain of the guard. Get twenty men assembled and ready within the hour." Phu-Bar glared at Finnochio with unmistakable intent. "Any questions?"

Finnochio swallowed hard and with a nervous quiver answered, "No, sir. It shall be as you ordered—twenty men within the hour."

"Excellent. I see I made the right choice for my new captain. Don't disappoint me." He left to tend to other affairs with his unspoken threat hanging in the air behind him.

As soon as Phu-Bar was gone, Finnochio whined with fear. "I don't want to be the captain. What happened to Moleinar? I thought he was the captain."

Peat was the one to say what they were all thinking. "Do you think he knows?"

Gropenhiney stood up and leaned forward with his hands on the table. "He might have found out about Moleinar, but I think that if he had even the slightest suspicion about any of us, we wouldn't be alive to discuss it right now."

Frank rubbed his scrawny chin thoughtfully. "It seems our best course of action would be to do as Phu-Bar says. Maybe, just maybe, this is our opportunity to carry out the next part of Apaula's—er, our plan."

Scotty did not try to conceal his rage toward Phu-Bar for threatening Finnochio's life. He placed his hand atop his lover's. "If he tries to hurt you, I'll kill him myself."

Finnochio flushed with pride at Scotty's bravado. He only wished that there was more time to properly demonstrate his appreciation for the sentiment.

Peat watched the exchange between the two men and swallowed his own dislike for their mating practices.

"We'd better get started rounding up those troops if you don't want to piss on the sentor's merciful mood."

"Good idea," Frank added.

"Let's go," Finnochio ordered, reluctantly shifting his thoughts back to the situation at hand.

CHAPTER 10

Sal pulled another in a seemingly endless succession of weeds from the garden plot. He stopped and stood up straight to stretch the aching muscles in his lower back. "Merda. I'm getting too old for this."

Sal grew up working the vineyards with his father back in the old country of Vespuccia and was used to the hard labor necessary to grow any kind of food crop. Consequently, he had grown into a middle-aged, short, stocky man with large muscular shoulders and a steel clasp for a grip. Those hands were now dirt black, as were his fingernails while his fingers had a decidedly green tint to them. Placing his hands in the small of his back, he arched over backwards to stretch. Gazing skyward with his kind brown eyes, a groan escaped his lips. "Oh, that feels good. But I think if I stay bent over any longer I might get stuck in this position."

Raziel smiled along with his friend at the empty complaint. He knew Sal didn't mind the work, and neither did he. It was satisfying his need to be doing something now that he and the captain were landlubbers. He also liked the rewards of watching the crops grow under his care, and of course eating them when the time was right.

Raziel was a large man with an appetite to match, and the rake he was working with looked toy-like in his big hands. At six-foot-three and nearly two-hundred-fifty pounds, he was a giant amongst most men, and most of it was hard muscle from years of being a sailor.

He stopped raking for a moment to commiserate with his friend. "Tell me something I don't know. This is hard work! I'd give anything to be back at sea with a sturdy ship beneath my heels. I was never one who loved toiling in the fields," he said half jokingly. He really missed being at sea, with a strong wind to his back, the feel of the ship beneath his feet as she rolled with the ocean swells, the squawk of seagulls and the crisp salt air just after a squall.

"Toil?" Sal said mockingly. "All you're doing is flapping your jaw." He tossed another weed onto his growing pile.

"Hmm," Raziel muttered as he gathered up the pile with a small wooden spade and hauled the unwanted greenery to a wooden bin off the far side of the barn. In the bin it would be left to rot with organic leftovers from their meals until it became rich in plant nutrients, at which time they would turn it back into the ground, replenishing the soil.

He returned to the garden where Sal had already started on a new pile of weeds.

"Hey, Sal. Have you ever stopped to think about what we're doing here?"

"I'm pulling weeds," Sal snapped tersely.

"That's not what I meant."

Sal sat back on his haunches and looked up at Raziel, "I know," he said somberly. "And, yes. I have given it some thought." He stood up and brushed his hands off on the legs of his trousers.

Raziel leaned on the spade and gazed off into the distance. "I've been thinking about our situation—about living here. And I'm not sure if settling down in this valley is what I'm ready to do."

Sal moved over to a sawed-off tree stump and sat beside his friend. "Yeah, I know what you mean. I've been wondering the same thing for myself."

"It's not that I don't appreciate what we have here. It's just. Well—" Raziel fumbled for the right words.

Sal completed the thought. "It seems as if we have something greater to be doing with our lives?"

"Yes, I think that's it," Raziel mused. "I felt much more alive with purpose when we were fighting for our very lives, first aboard ship and then later in that swamp where you almost became snake food."

"Don't remind me. Not that I could forget being clamped in the jaws of that bedeviled monster, but you know I think for once I agree with you. Living here as a farmer seems more like just passing the days until death. I yearn for some excitement."

Raziel rubbed the back of his neck as he spoke, "It's odd if you think about it. Here we are with everything we could need to live comfortable lives, yet I never felt more alive than at those times where I faced almost certain death."

Sal stood up from his stump and gently patted his friend on the back. "We should be more grateful for what we have and less desirous of that which we left behind."

"I suppose."

"You know the old saying—be careful what you wish for."

Raziel looked Sal in the eye. "Perhaps you're right," he said seriously. Then slowly an enormous grin spread across his face. "But I'll never admit it."

Sal smiled in return, "Come on. Let's get this garden weeded out before lunch."

"I'm with you," Raziel agreed as the two men returned to their respective tasks.

Across the yard, Laktos and Captain Caruso were busy splitting logs for firewood.

The captain was a stout man of medium height, with a portly build, and a large heart. His long white beard and hair, coupled with rosy cheeks and dancing eyes, gave him a grandfatherly appearance. His heavy sea coat and captain's hat, complete with large ostrich plumes, hung from a nearby fence post.

He wiped the sweat from his forehead with the back of his sleeve, then reached over to a pile of logs crosscut into two-foot lengths and hoisted another one up onto the chopping block.

Laktos waited until the captain stepped back, then swung his axe in a high arc, bringing it down with sufficient force to split the log in two halves. In the same manner, the two pieces were split again, and the quarters stacked onto another pile.

They had been working mostly in silence, with only an occasional word regarding the task at hand. Laktos had been thinking a lot lately about the captain, and finally decided it was time to talk about their future—or more pointedly, the captain's.

"Captain. I've been meaning to ask you something, and I'm not sure how to put it."

Caruso set down the log he was holding and sat down upon it. "Best to just speak your mind. What's troubling you?"

"Well. We've been living here nearly half a year, and it's never come up. But, well, I was wondering what your plans are. To be more specific, have you thought about returning to the sea?"

Caruso stared at a spot between his booted feet. "I'd be a liar if I said I didn't miss the ocean or my ship."

"Why haven't you ever spoken of it?"

Caruso looked up at Laktos. "The time never seemed right, I guess. But as of late, with spring in the air and summer rapidly approaching, it seems the thought has been on my mind more often than not."

Laktos set aside his axe and sat down beside his friend. "Inga and I have been discussing our future, and we've decided to stay here with John and Sienna. Maybe raise a family of our own."

"You'd be a fool not to. Inga's a fine woman."

"Of course, you'd be welcome to stay, too. I know Inga has a great fondness for you—possibly as deep as the love for her own father."

The sentiment touched the captain and found his voice had deserted him. He cleared his throat to empty away his choked-back emotions. "I've always looked to her and Yennek—may God rest his soul—as my own children. They were the family that I had always wanted, but could never seem to find the time to start, me being at sea so much. I guess that I'd always felt there would come a day far off in the future when I would find the right lass and settle down. Now it seems as if that day has passed me by."

"I hardly think so. You're not that old." Laktos continued, feigning a deadly serious look. "Although your ugly mug sure would be a test of genuine love for even the hardiest woman."

A slight smile played across the captain's lips. "No truer words were ever spoken."

A comfortable silence settled over the two men as each was lost in their own thoughts. Laktos softly broke the quiet with a single word that spoke volumes. "Well?"

The captain didn't answer Laktos' question, but instead asked one of his own. "You ever think about why we all were brought together?"

"Yes." Laktos was momentarily taken aback. For a reason he could not fathom, it had never occurred to him that the others would wonder about the same thing. "It does seem likely that some of us were 'guided' together. When I think back to Sal and Inga's story of the vagabond, it certainly sounds as though the same man had given them prophecy and a choice to make."

"I felt the same thing the first time I heard the tale. The similarities were too many for it to have been a coincidence. And yet how could it not be so? That thought has been bouncing around in my head for months," Caruso said, deep in thought. "If our fate is not our own, then what are we but puppets on a string? Puppets don't get a choice to make. Perhaps that's the difference between freewill and fate. We all made choices that brought us together in this time and place. There's no point in debating what would have happened had we chosen differently at any juncture in the past. The actual truth is what we have before us and the simple fact that we are all here despite the tremendous obstacles that we each had to overcome. It seems like a miracle, doesn't it? At times it seems that there must be some divine being who takes care of those of us with foolish hearts. It's for sure that I'd be swimming with the mackerels if not for Prometheus, and there'd be no dragon had you not saved him from the wizard Drang, and no saving him if I had chosen not to take you to Monad's island in the first place and—"

Laktos picked up the thought, "And you're making my head spin."

Caruso stopped his tirade and looked at Laktos. "You get my point."

"Yeah, but I guess." Laktos paused, searching for the right words to ease the captain's mind. "There are some things in heaven that mortal men should not know lest we forego our freewill and give up having a choice."

"You know. I think I'm beginning to see your perspective," the captain mumbled, deep in contemplation.

"Does that mean you're going to be staying here with us for a time?" Laktos asked, attempting to keep his voice as neutral as possible so he would not influence the captain's answer in any way.

The captain thought long and hard over what he should do. His choices were simple: stay here and live a life farming, or return to his first passion—the open sea. "I believe I should speak of this with Raziel before I make any kind of decision. I feel I owe it to him since he's the last of my original crew."

"Hard to be a captain without a crew," Laktos said warmly.

Before Caruso could speak, a beckoning call interrupted their conversation.

"Laktos! Come here, quick!" Sal shouted as he and Raziel waved to get his attention.

The captain looked over to see what all the fuss was about. "I wonder what's got him all fired up?"

"Let's go see," Laktos said curiously.

He took a step and was stopped as Caruso lightly grabbed his forearm.

"Thanks," Caruso said with a smile.

Laktos shrugged self-consciously, not entirely comfortable being at the receiving end of serious sentiments.

"No worries—what are friends for? Come on. Let's go see what Sal is up in arms about." Laktos stuck out his hand, which Caruso grasped firmly and stood up.

"Maybe it's a giant worm with big teeth." Caruso held his fingers up beneath his nose as if to portray a set of huge fangs. "Big teeth!"

Laktos laughed at the sight as he and the captain walked over to where Sal was. The smile slowly faded as he got nearer and saw the serious look on Sal's face. "What's going on?" he asked in a more sober tone.

Sal shushed him and pointed to the far corner of the garden.

Laktos saw nothing to cause such distress in his friend. "I don't see—"

Sal cut him off with a stern whisper, "The bird—look at the bird."

Laktos looked more closely and spied a small bird perched on a tree stump. It was mostly black with a small white plume of feathers on its breast. He had seen more than a few of the tiny avians on his journeys. "I still don't get—"

Sal punched Laktos in the arm. "How thick is your skull? Look what it has around one of its legs."

There, carefully secured around the fragile limb, was a circlet of gold holding what appeared to be a rolled-up scrap of paper.

"What on earth?" Laktos took a tentative step forward to see the object more clearly. The bird puffed out his wings, but did not try to fly away. Laktos took another step, then another, and still the bird stayed rooted to his perch. The nearer he got to the bird, the more familiar it seemed. He wracked his brain, trying to remember where he had seen it last. Then suddenly it came to him. That bird, or one just like it, had been squawking at him from the library rooftop where he had met the wizard librarian MOT.

Sal and the others watched in rapt silence as Laktos walked to within a few inches of the bird. They collectively held their breath as Laktos reached out for the small creature. Laktos gently cupped the bird in his hands. He could feel the frightened thumping of the birds' tiny heart, yet it made no move to escape. It seemed that even though it was frightened of him, it also trusted him beyond the fear. Carefully, so as not to injure the bird's leg, Laktos removed the gold band with the paper, then softly set the bird back on the stump.

The bird puffed out his chest and stretched his wings while shaking his tail feathers as if to say I'm glad that's done with. Then with a squawk it took to flight and quickly disappeared into the nearby treetops.

Sal, Raziel and the captain rushed over to Laktos and all started talking at once. "That was amazing!" Sal spat out.

"If I hadn't seen it with me own eyes, I'd swear you were a liar," Caruso said with unfettered awe.

"What's on the note?" Raziel asked—the one question on everyone's mind.

"Let's see." Laktos carefully unfolded the piece of paper and beheld a simple line written in a precise cursive.

"Well?!" the others asked in unison.

Laktos looked up from the note. His face was unreadable, but his eyes held a look of impending doom. "It says, 'Help. Come quickly! MOT'"

Chapter II

The barkeep looked around his half-darkened tavern as he wiped yet another well-used mug clean. He absently set it next to a dozen more of its kind lined up on the old wooden counter top. He lazily picked up the last tankard and with the same rag that he'd been using for the past two years, he "cleaned" out the vessel. When he was finished, he tossed the rag into a bucket of oily water that he kept under the bar. Then one by one he placed the mugs high on a shelf behind him. He watched the room and everyone in it as he worked. He was always wary and on guard. When his back was turned, he watched his patrons in a looking glass that hung beneath the shelf.

The crowd was small this early in the day, with only a half dozen of the village's most hardy drinkers imbibing on his best brew of the season. He was proud of this year's batch of ale and boasted loudly about his special barley, dung and limestone mix to anyone who would listen. The rest probably wished they were deaf.

Sifty didn't mind their ridicule—he knew they'd come back and spend their time and money at the "Hawk 'n Spit." Not because they liked his company or his usually harsh words. It was because he owned the only pub in town.

He casually eyed the group seated toward the rear. The seven of them sat together at a table in the corner and talked in hushed tones, as if they were afraid someone

147

might overhear their conversation. They had rushed in only minutes before, and by their furtive glances and nervous twitters, he thought that they might leave just as quickly.

Sifty knew them, as he did all his patrons. Their group usually came in every night and sat at that same table, plotting and scheming as if he had no clue about what they were up to. He idly wondered what had brought them in at such an early hour.

The only other patron was a filthy beggar of a man who slouched in slovenly splendor all alone at a table in the farthest corner of the pub. He sat back in deep shadow, quietly exuding the tangy aroma of unwashed human, drinking his ale steadily. Sifty vaguely recognized the old man when he had staggered in several hours before. He'd been a regular customer at one time, of that he was sure. Beyond that snippet, he could recall no more about the old sot.

The pub door swung inwards accompanied by a loud annoying screech the likes of which made the skin crawl down Sifty's back. He loved it. The din intruded upon the relative quiet of the tavern as the sound of fingernails clawing at black slate. Sifty, along with everyone else, cast their gaze toward the entrance.

The dark presidress entered the pub with her head down, her face hidden in shadow. The rickety door groaned as it slowly closed behind her. She remained absolutely still for the moment and breathed as she felt the eyes of everyone upon her. She was indifferent to their stares as she glided towards the bar.

Sifty assumed it was a woman by the petite shape, but the newcomer's cloak draped the slight form from head to toe and hid almost all but a glimpse of a delicately sculpted chin. His scrutiny of the newcomer was interrupted by a loud booming noise from the back of the room.

Apaula farted and cleared her throat to get the attention of her lackeys. Irritated with the interruption by the newcomer, she continued on with her intense questioning. "Tell me again what Phu-Bar said," she asked Finnochio quietly.

"He appointed me as the new captain of the guard and ordered me to assemble twenty men in just a little over a half hour from now."

Moleinar could hardly contain his rising anger. "You? Captain? Ha!"

Scotty tried to defend his lover. "He's capable of,"

"Of nothing!" Moleinar said scornfully. "If you two cowards had followed Phu-Bar and dealt with him in the forest as we had planned, then none of us would be in the dire positions we find ourselves." Moleinar glared at the group. It suddenly dawned on him the impact of Finnochio's new position. "If you're the new captain, then what is to become of me?"

Nikhole squirmed seductively on Gropenhiney's lap, which made him readjust his pressing position. "Maybe

you're going to be Phu-Bar's right-hand man?" she said
without thinking.

Moleinar should not have been surprised by his wife's
thoughtless comments, but he was beginning to see things
in a new light, realizing he was doomed. He looked at the
group of his so-called friends, his gaze falling upon his wife
as she sat perched atop Gropenhiney. A twinge of jealousy
passed through his bowels and he turned away. His gaze
found the stranger in the long cloak. She stood at the bar
with her back to him. He knew it was a woman, for no man
could have such delicately shaped curves. He wondered
what she would be like without clothes, if she would spend
time with him for what were probably going to be his last
hours on this earth. Moleinar had little doubt what Phu-Bar
had in store for him, and there was nowhere for him to run.
So why bother? He might as well try to enjoy what time he
had left.

He scarcely noticed when the others got up to fulfill
Phu-Bar's orders. The meaningless platitudes they
mumbled to him as they filed out brought him little solace.
Nikhole stepped between him and the object of his lust.
She bent down to give him a peck on the cheek, giving him
an unfettered view down her loose-fitting gown. He could
see between her large breasts all the way down her lithe,
naked body to her feet. "I'll be back in a little while," she
said. He hardly noticed her. She looked over her shoulder
at the reason for his distraction, then turned back to him.
Seeing his wanton lust for another woman angered her

more than just a little. He was supposed to be enticed by her attributes, even if she was sharing those attributes with another man at the moment. Not some faceless hag in an old robe. With an air of haughtiness, she turned on her heel and marched out of the pub. She'd show him. She was going to wear Gropenhiney out with her revenge.

Sifty could feel himself strangely attracted to this mysterious woman. The sensation scared him just a little. He tried unsuccessfully not to let his nervousness show. "What's your pleasure?" His voice sounded raspy to his ears.

"Two mugs of the house specialty, if you please." She spoke with a soft, seductive whisper—her voice full of sinful promise.

Sifty's heart skipped a beat at the sound of her voice. His hand trembled as he pulled the tap handle and filled her request. He tried to figure out why he was so nervous.

She laid three gold coins on the counter and reached for the drinks. Her hands were delicate and smooth. Her skin was the color of cream. As she bent forward, a sliver of her face was revealed in the dim lighting. Sifty caught his stomach in his throat. A glimpse of her face was more than he could take. So radiant was her beauty, he feared that any more of it would strike him completely senseless. She smiled ever so mischievously and turned away.

Sifty shook his head like a man waking from a dream. Now that her focus was elsewhere, he was feeling more like his old cantankerous self. "My eyes must be playing tricks on me." He reasoned it could not be her. Everyone knew the presidress had been burned to death several years ago. He caught himself staring at her as she walked across the room. He shook off the thought and poured himself a tall drink which he polished off in one swallow, then busied himself scrubbing the bar top with the ever-present rag.

Moleinar sat with his back to the presidress and glared under his brows at the empty tabletop. His thoughts again turned to the mysterious woman.

As if reading his thoughts, Presidress Lendura sidled up next to Moleinar's chair and spoke in a sensuous voice. "May I join you? I hate to drink alone and you look like you could use some company." Her question hung between them. With a drink in each hand, she allowed her robe to fall partly open. She watched his eyes bug out wide when he turned to see who it was that had interrupted his thoughts and beheld her semi-exposed nudity beneath.

Moleinar couldn't believe his good fortune as he stared open mouthed at the most beautiful woman that he had ever seen. He nearly fell from his chair as he clumsily tried to stand. "Please w-won't you sit here," he said, never once meeting her eyes as he hastily pulled the chair closest to him out for her.

"Thank you, sir. It's a proper gentleman that you are." She gave Moleinar a wink in return as she set the two drinks down and took the offered seat.

She twisted her lithe body into the waiting chair and turned it slightly towards his as she sat down letting her cloak fall open revealing a generous portion of her long slender legs.

Moleinar clumsily resumed his seat, unable to take his eyes from her perfectly proportioned legs. His eyes followed them all the way up until they disappeared beneath the folds of her robe. He gulped in nervous anticipation of what he could only imagine for the moment. But he sensed that this was only the beginning as he took a long refreshing drink from his cup of ale.

She daintily shifted herself very close to him and placed her hand upon his thigh. "I just love a man who knows how to treat a lady." She squeezed his thigh and ran her hand higher up his leg. "Are you that kind of man?" she whispered near his ear in a husky voice while her hand sought out his rising attention.

The siren's call of seduction rang in Moleinar's skull. His head spun as if from too much alcohol, and he could hardly focus his eyes.

Lendura rubbed his leg under the table and felt him tense with excitement. She knew all she needed to do was lead him, and he would surely follow like a lost puppy. "Why don't we go somewhere more secluded?" She leaned in very close to him and whispered her fiery breath into his ear. "Someplace where we can be alone."

He squirmed in his chair and could barely grunt out a "yes."

She gently squeezed his thigh then stood, wrapping herself once more within the confines of her cloak and made her way out of the pub.

Moleinar could not move fast enough. He hastily tossed a couple of brass coins on the bar and went out after his desire. He burst out of the pub and saw her shrouded figure waiting for him across the street. She beckoned him closer with barely a nod of her head. At that moment, he had eyes for her only. He took three steps, when suddenly his universe was filled with stars. He landed with a noticeable thud onto the cobblestone street, unconscious and oblivious to his broken nose and the extremely large welt on the back of his skull.

"You didn't have to hit him so hard. He could barely walk as it was," the presidress scolded.

Phu-Bar put on his best innocent face and shrugged his overly large shoulders. "I just wanted to be sure he didn't cry out," he said as he tried in vain to catch a glimpse of his master. He sensed something very different about her from their last encounter, but he couldn't quite place the feeling.

She scoffed. "Bring him to my chambers at once." She turned without another word and disappeared down an alleyway.

Phu-Bar watched her disappear into the midday shadows and noted that she seemed to walk straighter with a youthful spring in her step. "It must be my imagination."

He easily picked up Moleinar's limp form and tossed him none too gently into the back of a wooden cart. He threw a tattered burlap tarp over the unmoving form, then grabbed the halter of the single mule and her down the alley.

Chapter 12

Laktos stood in front of the hearth and looked at his friends seated around the log table in the den. Their collective faces all bore a look of expectation and curiosity as they impatiently waited for him to explain the mysterious note from MOT. He hardly knew where to begin. There was so much to tell and more that he dared not mention, even to these his trusted friends. Not even Inga knew the whole truth of his joining with the MOT machine and the secrets of the Ancients that it had shown him.

Inga sat silently to his side and waited to hear the words that she dreaded. She fought back the tears that threatened to burst from her eyes and tried not to think beyond the moment. Her thoughts were a beehive of doubts and insecurities mixed with her love for Laktos and a longing to see her family once more before they were only memories.

Sal could bear the silence no longer and uttered quietly, "What do you plan to do and how can we help?"

Laktos reached down and gently lay his hand on Inga's shoulder. She reached up and put her hand on his, gaining comfort from the show of affection.

Laktos spoke succinctly. "I have to go help MOT."

Inga's tears immediately started falling silently to the floor as her world fell apart. Her fears began the moment she saw the look in Laktos' eyes when he first entered the room carrying the note.

"That's settled," Sal announced supportively. "I'll get my sword and some supplies and we'll be off to see this wizard MOT."

The others all started talking at once, making plans for the expedition to the dead city. Inga already sensed what the others did not and held Laktos' hand tighter.

Laktos interrupted the group by stating flatly, "No."

A stunned silence settled over the room, broken at last by Caruso. "What do you mean?"

Sal piped up indignantly, "I know you're not going to start spouting off that 'I've got to go alone' speech again—as I recall, that nearly turned out to be your undoing on Monad's Island."

Raziel spoke his mind as well. "There is no force on this earth that will keep me from missing out on this adventure!" He had more to say, but paused when he saw the look of determination in Laktos' eyes.

Laktos waited until everyone was once again quiet. "My friends. I am deeply touched by your loyalty, but I made a promise to MOT, and I intend to keep it." He held his hand up to stave off any comments and then continued. "Truthfully, I do not want to go. Nor do I wish to leave Inga or the rest of you behind. But my word is my law, and I am honor bound to help MOT the same as I am to the likes of you." He looked down into Inga's upturned face and continued. "Would you have me be any other way?"

She knew that she would not, for it was that very quality of personal honor that had ensnared her heart from the beginning. She would change nothing about him. And knowing this, she had to make the ultimate sacrifice, putting aside her feelings and helping him as best she could. She gazed back into his beautiful eyes. "I understand," she said with a slight quiver in her voice. "I will get your things ready." She clenched his hand as he helped her up. She leaned in close and whispered in his ear. "I love you just as you are." Then she hurried off to their room to pack his supplies and to cry privately, undisturbed.

Captain Caruso spoke for the rest when he said, "Laktos. I understand that a promise is a promise, but what if you should need our help to save MOT from whatever this danger is? With us to watch your back—"

"All of you must understand. I cannot take you to the city of the dead. There is a danger there that I dare not expose you to. It's bad enough that I am burdened with this terrible knowledge, but I will not lay this burden upon you, my friends. Please don't ask me to."

Sal would not let Laktos off so easily. "I want the right to decide for myself if this knowledge is so terrible."

Laktos spoke quietly but firmly to his friend, "I'm afraid that your will is not the only one involved. MOT will not let you into the city, and he may even try to kill you to prevent your finding out what he does not want you to know."

"Damnable secrets!" the captain spat out. His outburst was directed at Laktos, but there was no anger in his tone—only intense frustration.

Sal turned to Raziel and smacked him smartly on the upper arm. "I warned you about the things you wish for," he said under his breath.

John, who had sat quietly in the back of the room with Sienna and the baby during the entire exchange, at last spoke up. "Since we can't go with you to the city, perhaps we could take you partway?"

Sienna was taken aback by John's use of the term we. She had no idea he had even considered going. Since when was he a fighter. "All this male posturing must have boiled your brain," she thought to herself.

Laktos considered John's offer only a moment before making his decision. "I think it would be best if only John and I go."

"So be it, then," the captain stated with the voice of authority that left no room for any more dissension. "Raziel. Let's you and I get the wagon out and Hansel hitched up. Sal and John will help Laktos load any supplies or weapons needed for his journey." In a kinder tone, he directed his next question to Sienna. "Sienna. Could you and Inga please prepare some dried meats and other staples for Laktos?"

"Yes, captain," Sienna readily agreed, and went in search of Inga.

The captain and the others all filed out to tend to their various tasks, leaving Laktos standing momentarily alone in an empty room. The ending that he had felt coming was upon him, and he knew in his heart that he would never see this place again. Though he couldn't explain the feelings of foreboding that he had, he could not deny them either.

He gazed around the quaint room and felt the memories of the last few months wash over him. In his mind he could hear their laughter and see the smiling faces of those few people in this life who he cherished warmed by the glow of the fire.

A great sadness slowly crept into his soul as he realized with infinite sorrow that all of those good days were gone and only his memory of them would carry on. But even that was not entirely true. The wizard Drang had spoken to him of another time and place where he had led a completely different life—a former life that he remembered only when he slept.

A sharp pain erupted in his right temple and ceased all his thoughts. He rubbed at the spot with his fingertips until the pain faded slowly away and decided that he had wracked his brain enough for one day. Hearing Inga and Sienna coming, he quickly masked his discomfort behind a sheepish grin.

Inga's arms were loaded with extra clothing, his sword, belt and various animal skin pouches. She laid them on the table without meeting his eyes and then went into the kitchen to help Sienna pack some dried foodstuff.

Laktos knew she was trying to avoid anything that would start her crying again, so he said nothing that would upset her. Instead, he methodically began to don his gear, starting with his belt pouches and finishing up by slipping his scabbard over his left shoulder and securing it to his waist belt. He reached back over his right shoulder and found the bone handle exactly where it should be. He gripped the haft and pulled the high carbon steel blade from its sheath and admired the deathly beauty of the killing tool. The mirrored finish of the steel held his gaze for a moment, then he returned the sword to its scabbard with practiced ease. Silently he hoped that he would have no need for the weapon, but inwardly he already had his doubts. He checked the foot-long dirk on his left hip and the dagger he kept in his left boot. With his preparations done, he gathered up his cloak and made his way outside to see how the others were doing.

Inga could hold back her tears no longer. Sienna stopped what she was doing and wrapped her arms around Inga and hugged her close. Inga wept openly into Sienna's shoulder. "I can't bear the thought of him leaving, yet I can do nothing to stop him from going."

Sienna just held Inga and quietly listened for the moment.

"Oh, God. What am I to do?" she cried.

"It'll be all right. He will be all right. You know that he's perfectly capable of defending himself from any danger." Sienna gently stroked the back of Inga's head. "I know

162

because I've seen him. I'll never forget how he saved my family from those murdering thieves. I swear that I thought that my life was over as I watched John nearly slain and awaited the horrors of what would come next. And then suddenly out of nowhere was Laktos. Like an avenging angel, he destroyed the bastards that had threatened us."

Inga had quieted and was now resting comfortably in the arms of her friend. "It's funny, but that's sort of how I met him. Not exactly, mind you, for I was in no danger. But the part of how he just happened to show up at the right time." She spoke softly between muffled sniffles. "If not for him, then the captain and Raziel would not be here. That much is certain. But why him?" Inga continued. "I mean, hasn't the world asked enough of him already?" Her frustration was plainly evident in her voice. "For the first time in my life, I'm completely at peace, and yet it seems sometimes as if there is something missing in my life. I don't really know what it is. When I look into his eyes and feel the warmth of his soul, I have no doubt about where I should be, and that is at his side. But lately I've found that if he is away, my heart withers from starvation, and I can feel my soul drifting towards a new destiny. I just don't feel happy and I'm not sure why—I'm not even certain about Laktos anymore."

"You mustn't say that," Sienna said reprovingly. "I don't pretend to understand why things happen the way they do, but I must believe that there's a good reason for you two to be together. You just have to believe in the love you profess to each other and know that as long as you hold on to that promise, there will be more happiness yet to come."

Inga slowly pushed away from Sienna and wiped her tears away with the hem of her skirt. "Yes, I suppose that you're right," she said at last, resigned to a course of action. "Besides, there seems nothing I can do about it."

"You could pray for his safe return."

Inga didn't answer, but she had one thought, "What about me?"

"I know he will be back," Sienna said attempting to ease Inga's mind.

For a fleeting moment, their gaze met and Sienna could see a glimmer of something in Inga's tear-moistened eyes that gave her pause. An emptiness that sent shivers down her spine. "Come along. Let's finish packing this food. It'll take your mind off things, if only for a wee bit."

With a childlike resignation in her voice, Inga replied, "Sure," and somberly went back to work. In a short time, they had all the food and supplies Laktos could carry, nearly a two-week ration divided between two deer-hide pouches.

"I think I'm ready," Inga said. She put on her bravest face and opened the door.

Caruso barely restrained himself from hitting Raziel, "The ass end of the mule goes at the other end of the harness."

"What do you know about donkey carts? I thought you were a ship's captain!" Raziel snapped in frustration as he tried to control a very stubborn mule.

"I am, or was. But it's my captaining of asses that tells me that something is amiss around here!"

"I'll gladly trade places with you," Raziel grunted as Hansel whipped his head around and nearly shook himself free of his grasp.

Laktos entered the barn. "Is there a problem?" he said with obvious humor at Raziel's expense.

As if to answer him, Hansel brayed loudly in protest of Raziel's clumsy attempts at hitching him to the wagon harness.

"What are you complaining about?" Sal said as he carried a full water bladder over from the well and placed it in the back of the wagon.

"Nothing that a jug of rum couldn't cure," Caruso answered under his breath.

Caruso ran the bridle leads around Hansel's flanks and finished making the connections that hitched Hansel to the wagon. "There. That should do it."

Hansel playfully nipped at the captain's arm while swishing his tail about in eager anticipation of his awaiting task.

Together, the four men guided Hansel and the wagon out of the barn without further incident.

John walked over a moment later and casually inspected their work. Seeing that all was in readiness, the men waited in awkward silence for Inga and Sienna to arrive with the foodstuffs and other supplies that Laktos required for his long journey.

Sal found the silence too much to bear and so he paced back and forth, his frustration clear by the sour expression on his face and the speed at which he was going nowhere.

Laktos wore a look of bemused concern as he watched his friend and waited. He had seen Sal get worked up like this on more than one occasion and had eventually learned that it was best to leave him be, for now.

"He looks like a primed cannon," Caruso said to no one in particular. "Ready to blow a hole in someone's day."

"More like a strutting rooster," John said dryly. "Look how his head bobs around."

Raziel made an overacted non-physical study of Sal as if he were the subject for a scientific analysis of the modern Vespuccian, when suddenly he smacked himself in the forehead and said aloud, "Yes, I see it too! It's definitely a bird thing." He bobbed his head back and forth on his shoulders to emphasize his words.

Sal just glared at him as he walked past. "Go ahead, make jokes—meanwhile am I the only one who has a sense of forebod—" he stopped himself from saying anything more. No matter what he felt, he wasn't going to voice aloud his fears and make the situation worse. "Pay no mind to me. I'm just shooting off my big mouth."

Raziel felt some regret for having teased his friend, not realizing that Sal had been so deeply affected by the current events. He heard the cabin door open and saw Inga and Sienna coming out and was grateful for the interruption.

Inga and Sienna stepped out of the cottage, each with a small armload of supplies and walked over to where the others were waiting by the wagon. Laktos relieved Inga of her burden, and together they walked a short distance from the others. She looked up into his face, her eyes glistening with tears. "Oh Laktos—" Her voice failed her and she could hold back the tears no longer. She buried her face in his broad chest and wept.

He held her tight with his cheek upon her head and choked back the powerful emotions that flooded his mind. He felt weary of his heavy burden for having to leave and wanting more than anything else not to go. "I'm sorry, Inga. I don't want to go."

Inga's grief flared into sudden anger as she snapped quietly at him in reply. "Then don't. You don't have to go. Let the world take care of itself!" she demanded.

"You know I can't do that."

"But why?" she pleaded.

"I have to live my life under my own terms, Inga, if I am to be the man that I am. I made a promise and I intend to keep it."

"Don't I matter to you?"

"Of course you do. It's—"

"It's what?" she flashed. "That MOT is more important than me? Is that it?" Her eyes burned with anger.

"No. You're the most important person in the whole world to me—I love you," he said in a choked voice. He felt slightly overwhelmed by the stress of leaving and Inga's emotional outburst. "Why can't you understand?"

She held him tighter. "I'll not let you go!" She stood her ground like a petulant child.

"Inga, please. I must. There simply is no other choice for me. I swear to you that I will return as quickly as possible." He placed his hand beneath her chin and gently turned her face up so he could look into her tear-filled eyes. "I swear it. I love you, Inga."

She couldn't bear to see the look of determination in his eyes and looked away. "No," she whispered. "No, I won't wait here in torment day after day, always looking down that road to see if you're on the way home."

Laktos heart skipped a beat. "What are you saying?"

Inga met his gaze.

He recognized a stubborn, childlike look of hurt and anger in her bloodshot eyes. "Inga—"

"If you leave me now, I won't be here when you get back," she retorted. She knew she was backing herself into a corner trying to force him to stay with her, but like a rock rolling down a steep slope, she could not stop herself. "Maybe you should go back to the presidress in your dreams—she seems to be calling you from the past!" With her emotions running away with her, she said anything that came to mind no matter how illogical it sounded.

Laktos felt his world slipping away. "How can you say that?"

"Why do you still dream of her if you don't love her anymore?"

"I could no more control what I dream any more than I can remember my past. You're not being fair. Inga, I beg you, don't make me have to choose between you and my promises."

She pushed away from him. "You promised to love me!"

"And I do. Every day that I'm with you. Can't you see that?"

She answered as if she had not heard him. "So what you're saying is you no longer love me if you should choose to go to MOT?"

"I never—"

"So, make your choice—it's me or MOT." She gathered up the hem of her skirt and ran into the cabin, sobbing uncontrollably.

Sienna gave John a look that said he'd better not side with Laktos, then followed Inga a moment later.

Laktos stood rooted to the spot, unmoving. His heart thundered in his chest, fueled by the anguish that threatened to tear his soul apart. He wanted to follow her into that cabin and hold her in his brawny arms. Kiss her soft, warm lips, smell the fragrance of her hair and make love to her with all of his being. Instead, a deep lonely sigh escaped his mouth as he slowly turned towards John and his waiting friends. They all suddenly looked elsewhere, and comically they made themselves busy doing nothing as Laktos approached. Without a word, he climbed up on the wagon and waited silently for John to climb up next to him and take the reins. He looked down at the captain, Raziel and Sal "Take care of her for me, please. I'll come back as soon as I can. And tell her that I love her."

"I think she already knows that," Sal said.

"She'll wait for you Laktos," Caruso said trying to give comfort to his friend. "Women just get confused sometimes, that's all."

Laktos kept his silence and merely nodded his reply. He looked at each of his friends as if he were fixing their images in his mind. Somehow, he had the feeling that he might never see any of them again. "Take care of each other."

With a slap of the reins, John urged Hansel forward and the trio started off up the mountain road.

Inga watched from their bedroom window. Tears flooded down her flushed cheeks and soaked their pillow with her heartache. Deep inside, she felt the first faint clasp of barrenness that was replacing her love for him with confusion and emptiness.

Laktos and John rode in silence up the mountain side, neither man knowing what to say to the other. John's thoughts revolved around all the strange events as of late and the new direction that everyone's lives had suddenly taken. Odd how yesterday life at the farm had the feeling of perpetuity and today how it was all so different, so final in its ending.

Laktos stared blankly off into the distance. Every once in a while, the trees would open out and he could see the farmhouse ever so tiny down in the valley below. He saw Inga in his mind's eye the last time they had run through the meadow together with her hair flying in the breeze. She had seemed so happy with him, so in love with him, and yet scarcely days later she would walk away from their lives thinking only of her wants. What other way could he have shown her how much he cared if not by simply being there with her every moment of their lives. What greater expression of love than to want to be with her. What greater pain could he feel to know that she no longer wanted to be with him, that somehow being with him wasn't enough for her any longer? He felt a tightness close around his chest and his heart fluttered under the strain of his pent-up emotions. He held them in, bottled them up in a place where he had buried the past.

The sky had grown cloudy by the time they reached the crossroads, and the threat of rain hung heavy in the air. Laktos jumped down and retrieved his gear from the rear of the wagon. He walked back around the front where John was standing next to Hansel. He laid his hand upon

171

Hansel's side and gave the old mule a gentle pat, "You take care, you old hay burner." Hansel brayed in response.

John extended his right hand in the traditional fashion. "Take care of yourself, Laktos."

Laktos clasped John's hand in a firm grip. "Until tomorrow we shall meet again, my friend." He shouldered his pack and started off down the road. Laktos walked a few yards, then turned and waved a last goodbye to John and Hansel as they started back down the mountain to the place he used to call home.

A great weariness passed through his body as he turned away from the life that he left behind, and with shaky legs he started to walk down the rocky road towards a new destiny. His heart felt like a ball of lead in his chest as he thought about Inga and her promise to not wait for him. How she could be so short-sighted and selfish about their relationship was a mystery to him and it shattered his whole belief about the love that she professed. It was his belief that love didn't stop when you didn't get your own way. It was supposed to be eternal through whatever life offered— the good times and to him, the more important hard times that befall everyone sooner or later. Her promise to leave him at this time in his life when he needed her most was heartbreaking. Worse than that, in his mind was how much it brought forth a remembered pain from somewhere in his forgotten past. The combined torment split his soul and caused anguish in his physical body that nearly stopped him in his tracks. His skull felt as if it would burst from the pressure. It was all he could do to keep moving forward, one trembling step at a time.

The present and his forgotten past collided within his mind. His feet faltered as a sob of absolute sorrow escaped unbidden from his clenched jaws. It was a cry born of complete and total despair, the last echoing forlorn cry made by someone facing imminent death and begging for just one more minute of life. Somewhere off in the rain-darkened forest, a wolf howled in answer to his lonely wail.

The sky opened up, and the rain began to fall. He turned his face to the heavens and let the downpour wash the streaming tears from his eyes. Distant thunder pealed across the heavens in rhythm to the beating of his breaking heart. He meandered, unthinking, unfeeling of anything except the raindrops that splashed down upon his face.

Gray and black clouds swirled over his head in a pattern that seemed familiar—one that he surely would have recognized had he been able to think about anything except Inga and how much he already missed her. Still, he knew he could not go back and the brutal truth was as soon as she had said that she would leave him, he knew in his heart that she was already gone.

With a heavy sigh, he resolutely continued on down the muddy road. Without genuine love to bolster him, he felt abandoned in his heart—solo on his journey to seek the meaning of his life. His was a world of darkness with no light to show him the way out.

Chapter 13

Phu-Bar dumped Moleinar's unconscious form in the presidress' dungeon. After chaining him to the wall, he hastily made his way back outside. He told himself that he hurried because he wanted to meet his guards and set out immediately in search of Laktos. The truth was, the dungeons made him very uncomfortable. He didn't enjoy being so far underground—the air seemed thicker somehow and was stifling, hard to breathe. It was as though he could feel the oppressive weight of all those tons of dirt and rock bearing down on him, suffocating him.

Once outside in the fresh air, he felt better. He stood in the shade of the crumbling wall and waited for the hammering in his chest to abate. Before him lay a weed-infested courtyard that had once, long ago, boasted a bountiful garden which encircled an inviting pond. The pond was nothing but a dusty depression in the earth with no evidence that it had ever been anything else.

An old memory flashed before his eyes. He saw himself standing on the far side of the courtyard with the presider. He was laughing at something he had said, and this unwanted memory actually had him smiling with nostalgia for a time before the presidress and his treachery—a time when he had been proud to be considered a friend by the presider. But that time was past. He clamped down on his feelings and bottled them up in that other place, the place in his mind where he dared not go.

Angrily he strutted his way through an open archway and turned left towards the horse stables. The stable house was an immense structure that at one time held upwards of fourteen trusted steeds. A year past, most of the structure and a third of the roof had collapsed in on itself during a violent storm, the likes of which no one had ever seen before or since. By some miracle, the only two horses still in the building had been spared any harm, as their end of the barn had survived the storm's fury.

Phu-Bar moved cautiously past the first stall and tried to peer into its shadowy depths. The lighting was poor and he could just barely make out the silhouette of its lone occupant standing far in the recesses of the barn. On the horse's forehead was a white blaze in the shape of a crescent moon, which seemed to glow with a supernatural light in the darkened stall.

Kamir stared out of his gloomy barn and shifted his hooves nervously. He tasted the scent of something evil in the air. He snorted and tossed his head as he recognized this particular human. This was the one who had been there the day his human friend had perished. With his tail held up in defiance, he pranced in circles within the confines of his stall. He did not like this human and showed his feelings by whinnying, snorting and tossing his head about. His nostrils flared wide and his ears lay flat against the side of his head in anger.

Phu-Bar watched the horse with a mixture of admiration and loathing. He wanted nothing more than to conquer this proud beast, to show it that he was the master now. But the damned horse would let no one get near him other than the grizzled old groundskeeper who had cared for him ever since the presider's death. Thinking of the old man, Phu-Bar abruptly noticed his absence. He looked left and right, but there was no sign of the man, by sight or smell. He shrugged the groundskeeper's absence off and figured the old coot was probably drunk somewhere or sleeping it off.

Phu-Bar had a sudden thought. Wouldn't it make an impressive statement to his troops if he were to show up riding Kamir? The prestige of riding the ex-presider's mount would bolster his commanding presence before his men. It would serve him well to demonstrate his dominance of the realm and all of its occupants, human or otherwise. He moved closer to the stall door. "It has been too long since you've been out."

Kamir shied to the back of his stall as Phu-Bar neared. He nodded his head up and down, snorting as he did so while pawing at the dirt with his front hooves. His tail thrashed wildly around with a whip-like swoosh of air.

The more Phu-Bar thought about riding the presider's steed, the more the idea appealed to him. He would lead his forces from atop the noble beast and show his men just how powerful a leader he was. He released the latch and slowly opened the stall gate. Kamir heard the latch release and watched the gate begin to swing open. He saw his chance to be free and with his head down he bolted towards the opening and Phu-Bar.

Phu-Bar shoved off of the gate and dove out of the charging horse's path with only a hair's breadth separating him from the fleeing steed. Kamir ran as fast as his four hooves would carry him. He cleared the gate before it had a chance to swing back shut and sprinted for the trees. In seconds, he disappeared into the forest where he ran and ran and ran.

Phu-Bar shakily stood up and brushed at the dirt that clung to his clothes. "One day, I'll kill that blasted horse and feed him to the peasants." He hobbled over to the other stall and looked at the pathetic gray nag stabled within. Her back was so bowed that he felt he could probably drag his feet once saddled upon her. Her head hung low, and she radiated an aura of total and complete laziness as she idly munched on bits of straw. She offered him no resistance as he led her out of the stall and tied her to a hitching rail. Phu-Bar had no problems getting her tacked up and in short time he was headed back to town and his waiting guards. Had the old gray mare plodded along any slower, she might have started moving backwards. As it was, he probably could have crawled faster than her lethargic pace. He heeled her sides to get more speed out of her, but she paid him no mind and continued on at her own pace.

Finnochio paced nervously back and forth in front of the assembled guards. He had gathered only eighteen of the twenty men that Phu-Bar had requested, and he was terrified of what the sentor's reaction might be to his perceived failure. He repeated his excuses over and over to himself, but they did nothing to ease his fears.

Finnochio glanced once again at the wagon that brought up the rear of the column. Loaded in the back was one of the town's cannons, along with a keg of powder and several different types of shot. He hoped that the extra firepower would distract Phu-Bar from the shortage of men. He spied Scotty at the reins of the wagon with Gropenhiney sitting beside him. Frank and Peat rode in the back.

The sound of an approaching horse caught his ear, and he turned to see Phu-Bar riding up on an old nag of a horse. He thought it best not to make a point of his shortcomings to Phu-Bar. Instead, he simply stated, "The men are ready to go at your order, sentor."

Phu-Bar let his gaze roam over the group. "We'll march in two columns with the captain leading. Our first stop will be at the crossroads near the top of the pass." He looked at Finnochio. "Let's move out." He moved his horse to the side of the road and watched as the columns of men marched past.

Finnochio was so grateful that the sentor had not even bothered to count the troops that he eagerly assumed the lead position. He nearly skipped down the road, so great was his relief. The troop of guards reluctantly followed their swishing new leader up the long dusty road toward their destination. Most of them wondered what had become of their actual captain, Moleinar, and harbored serious doubts about their new leader's capabilities. Some might have fled their duty had it not been for Phu-Bar trailing up the road behind them.

Phu-Bar trailed them just far back enough to avoid the cloud of dust that engulfed his men. He was still close enough to shout out orders if need be, but far enough away that should they be caught in an ambush, he would have ample time to escape.

The nag held a steady pace with little urging. Before long Phu-Bar felt himself get into the rhythm of the horse's gait and relaxed in the saddle.

His thoughts wandered aimlessly until they eventually came round to his current predicament. He savored the idea of finally catching Laktos and putting an end to the persistent rumor that he was his old friend the presider. A nagging doubt crept in to his musing, but what if he was?

He tried to imagine how it would feel to see his old friend the presider alive again. Unbidden memories of the many joyous times they had spent in revelry flashed through his mind. He probably should have felt some pang of remorse and loss, but instead only a cold hollow anger remained in his heart.

A guilty heart will bury the unconscionable truth, and he knew the truth about the presider's so-called accident. He had watched his friend drown with his own eyes, had turned his back in refusal of the hand that had reached out to his friendship for help.

No. Laktos was not the presider, but he would have to die never-the-less along with all who knew of him.

The sky held scattered thunderclouds that floated serenely past. The smell of rain hung heavy upon the spring day. In the distance, Phu-Bar could see a gray curtain below a black cloud. Lightning flashed within the isolated storm, followed a few seconds later by the sound of thunder.

The surrounding forest was alive with a plethora of birds all singing loudly in warning of the coming deluge. The melodious sound was lost upon the murderous troop as the procession slowly made its way up the mountain and ever closer to the crossroads.

CHAPTER 14

Laktos trudged along, following the muddy lane. His body was numb from the chilly rain that had soaked his clothing. Had he the will to care, he could have donned his cloak and been dry and warm. His eyes were downcast with a vacant, withdrawn stare. His outward appearance mirrored the turmoil that burned in his brain.

He agonized over Inga and her decision to— "To what?" he grumbled to himself. He really had no idea what she was going to do. Would she really leave him or would she be there waiting for him to return? He hated the unfairness of the situation. She acted toward him as if he had intentionally made MOT summon him. He didn't want to leave her, did not want this responsibility thrust upon him by MOT. He wanted only to live in peace with Inga and their friends and grow old together. Now it seemed he would have none of those things.

Angered flared within him. He shouted up to the heavens, "Why me?! Why?!" His anguished cry went unanswered as he fell to his knees in the middle of the muddy road. He clasped his hands tightly together. Muscular tremors overwhelmed his already shuddering body. Tears welled in his eyes before falling with the rain to the earth. Thoughts and images flashed before his mind's eye. A part of his psyche watched the unbidden memories as if they were from another person. But the part of him that was his conscious self, reeled back in shock as image after image sparked intense feelings of remembrance within him. The past and the present collided within his mind and exploded outwards in the only way that his body could handle the tremendous mental stress taking place within. His stomach emptied its contents as he collapsed onto his side in the mud.

He hovered on the edge of consciousness for nearly an hour while his subconscious and conscious mind battled to organize the conflicting memories stored within his mind and bring some logical rationale to an otherwise irrational situation.

The steady rain that drummed down upon him kept him from slipping away into oblivion. Ever so slowly, his mind returned from his inner hell to the outer world. After what seemed an eternity, he convinced himself that it was necessary for him to get up out of the mud and take steps to heal his body. He had to continue living despite himself, not because he desired to, but because he simply had no other choice. Eventually a wagon would come along and run him over. Probably one hauling manure, he thought wryly. That he decided was not the way he wanted to meet his end.

The pile of clumped mud in the road slowly morphed into the shape of a man as Laktos once again faced his realm of nightmares and achingly stood up. With slow, deliberate steps, he set out on his journey. Although he was still emotionally in turmoil, he instinctively sensed there was daylight streaming into the well of darkness he suffered in. This ray of light gave him a modicum of hope. A sad smile touched the corner of his mouth as he realized that hope was all he had left in this world. That and a strange wizard named MOT who for reasons unknown had befriended Laktos.

As he continued to walk, his spirits began to rise. For in truth, they had no other direction to go. Eventually, his mind cleared enough that his thoughts turned toward MOT and his reason for being at this juncture in his life. He pondered MOT's message, once again trying to discover any hidden meaning, glean just a little more from the cryptic note. But the words told him nothing more than the obvious sense of urgency and perhaps desperation in MOT's plea for help.

He picked up his pace a little as his body warmed and worked out the stiffness and aches. It wasn't long before he came to his marker stones piled a few feet off the roadside to his left. It seemed a lifetime ago that he had made that pile. He had yet to save Sal, find that damnable island or to meet Inga.

With a sense of loss, he made a supreme effort to focus his thoughts outward onto his surroundings. He slipped through a hedgerow that formed a natural barrier following the course of the roadway. Once through he immediately located the old slab-stone pathway which wound its way through the woods towards the destination that he sought and continued on his way.

Laktos followed the intermittent trail through a plush forest filled with tall, majestic trees, their trunks sheathed in white bark. Their branches were heavy with broad green leaves that fluttered in a slight breeze. The rain clouds had parted for the moment, and golden sunlight glistened and sparkled in the rain-dappled foliage.

Laktos moved quietly but quickly through this part of the forest. The natural beauty which surrounded him lifted his spirits, but only slightly. As he walked away the miles, he tried to put into words to the feelings of nostalgic familiarity that the forest stirred in him. He knew it was more than his having been this direction before. It felt more reminiscent of something closer to a long, forgotten memory that danced teasingly at the brink of remembrance. The harder he tried to focus in on the memory, the farther away it seemed to go, until at last it faded from his mind's eye completely to be replaced by the steady pounding of his heartbeat.

Laktos stopped walking and gently rubbed his throbbing temples with his fingertips. "What the hell is wrong with me?" he thought without realizing he had spoken the words aloud. The pain slowly ebbed. "MOT said I had a vacuous brain with a five-year gap—whatever that is." He thought about having just spoken aloud to himself. "Well, that's it then. I'm going daft talking to myself."

The gentle woodlands soon gave way to a forest of gnarled trees that marked the entrance to the willow's tunnel. Ahead of him, the forest grew dark and forbidding.

The trail that he had followed disappeared into the darkness of the woods ahead. "Damn! How could I have forgotten this place?" he muttered under his breath.

Heavy blankets of pale webbing draped across the trailhead like funeral shrouds. Still more webbing covered every surface in endless layers as far as he could see down the arborous tunnel which wasn't very far at all. He hated this part of the trail. If ever he had wanted to know what a fly might feel like in a spider's house, this was it.

He mustered up his courage and reminded himself that he had passed this way three times before without incident. He could only hope that this time would prove to be no different as he hacked his way through the thick curtains of webbing with his sword.

His skin crawled with goose bumps as he slashed his way along the old stone-crete pathway. Sweat beaded on his brow as he struggled along wondering all the while how the arachnid stuff could become so thick again. It hadn't been that long ago since he had been here—or had it?

The air was eerily still with an undercurrent of expectation, of something unseen but all seeing, lurking in the shadowy ghosts of web-mantled trees.

The muffled snap of a twig off to his right brought him to a stop. His heart thundered in his ears as he strained to hear any sound while he scanned the forest for movement. His visibility was limited by all the cottony webbing that seemed to go on forever. The willow forest was unearthly silent, as if it too was holding its breath in fear. Laktos stood frozen in place and waited. An icy shiver started at the base of his spine and slowly traveled up to the nape of his neck, a shiver born from a primeval fear. He could scarcely breathe as thousands of years of human evolution screamed at him to flee for his life.

A muted clicking sound came from behind him. He spun around with his sword held ready to strike, but he could not see the source of the noise.

Suddenly, he felt a strong desire to run, to escape in any direction. He fought the urge to bolt in panicked flight and forced himself to continue on his way. With as little noise as possible, he hacked his way through the sticky webbing that crisscrossed the trail.

Every few seconds he looked back over his shoulder, convinced that he was being followed by something. The crawling sensation up his spine was vibrating madly with instinctual warnings of danger.

Again, the strange clicking noises came from somewhere behind him. He strained to see something, anything. He looked in every direction unable to quell the rising fear within him.

He looked up and choked back a cry of startled fear as his terror-filled brain tried to make sense of what his eyes were showing him. Suspended from a branch was a man staring down at him. It took a moment for Laktos to realize that the glassy orbs that gazed at him were devoid of any life.

The corpse was wrapped in a tight cocoon of webbing that allowed only the face to remain uncovered. The skin that showed was dried like a piece of old leather—in fact the whole corpse looked shrunken in on itself, as if drained of all sustenance inside out and all that remained was the husk of the man.

The sudden insight of how this person had died, the life literally sucked from his living body revolted Laktos. An involuntary shudder raced through his bones, as if the temperature had dropped by fifty degrees.

Click. Tap. Scrape.

The sound spurred Laktos to break out of his stupor of fear. With new found energy, he slashed through the webbing as fast as he could wield his sword.

Click. Tap. Scrape.

The sounds were definitely getting closer. He did not know how far he still had to go before he reached the clearing of the Ancients, and relative safety. From the way things were looking, he didn't think he was going to get that far. He decided to make a stand where he was rather than be attacked by surprise from behind. He turned with his sword raised, ready to face the unknown. His heart stopped beating as he stared at the most hideous creature he had ever seen moving rapidly towards him on eight hairy legs.

It moved with incredible agility for its size, easily as tall as a man and twice that in width of body. The head and pincer like jaws looked powerful enough to rip a man in half with little effort. Behind those formidable mandibles were two huge globular eyes that protruded from the skull in grotesque sacks of yellowish fluid. Inhuman eyes that glared at him hungrily as the creature quickly closed the distance between them.

Laktos noticed all that and more as he stood frozen in place—his body stunned with a primitive fear of arachnids ingrained into the memory of his cells. Although he remained outwardly unmoving, inside his brain was screaming at him to do something, anything to be away from this abomination that kept coming relentlessly towards him.

This was like some kind of nightmare that he wished he would awaken from soon. His limbs felt drained of strength; weak from debilitating fear. Laktos' feet were rooted to the spot, unable to run. His heart refused to pump the blood frozen in his veins, no air was inhaled to replenish his lungs. The entire world seemed to have frozen— everything except the damnable beast that held him mesmerized.

It was nearly upon him when it spewed forth a stream of viscous liquid webbing. Laktos reflexively jumped to the side to avoid the repulsive substance. The sticky goop stuck to a tree trunk with a sickening wet slap.

Spurred to action more out of stark fear than reasoning, he lashed out at the monster with his sword. With a swift downward stroke, he severed the left front leg from the carapace. Using the momentum from his swing, he spun himself away from the creature just inches from its snapping mandibles.

The swiftness of the beast startled him and he stumbled back a couple of steps in retreat. He barely got his sword up for another strike but had to hold back and retreat further as the arachnid pressed the attack. It was all he could do to block the beast's attempts to bite him as he continued to be pressed farther back along the trail.

The webbing that spanned the pathway was entangling him in its sticky strands. He realized suddenly that he would soon be trapped just as effectively by them as the spray from the monster's mouth. Evidently that was the spider's plan as it continued to press him further into the webs.

An image of himself suspended in a cocoon while the monster fed from his living body at its leisure flared through his brain and sent a fear-induced surge of adrenalin flooding through his veins. With a strength he would normally not possess, he flung himself forward with a fierce cry.

The actions of its prey momentarily stunned the spider. This was something that had never happened in its experience. The spider seemed to look at Laktos as if he'd lost his mind, which in a way he had. But whatever the reason, that split second was all the opening he needed as he drove all thirty-three inches of his high carbon steel blade into the creature's hairy torso.

He pulled the blade out with a gush of greenish-yellow gore and plunged it in again and again. He did not stop until the trembling of his fatigued limbs could no longer carry out his bloodlust and he was forced to halt from exhaustion. The spider thing was clearly dead, but even in death, it evoked evil and inspired fear.

Laktos stumbled a few steps away from the thing to catch his breath and regain some of his sapped strength. Slowly the strain of his ordeal subsided somewhat and his energy level returned to something closer to normal, although he was still weary from the battle. He was just about ready to continue on his way when something caught his attention.

Click. Tap. Scrape.

"No, it can't be—" he said under his breath. Quickly he slashed his way forward down the trail. He resisted the urge to look back over his shoulder, knowing that precious seconds could make the difference in this life-or-death race to the Ancients clearing. He knew that his only hope of survival lay with that mysterious place. All he had to do was reach it alive.

Click. Tap. Scrape. Click. Tap. Scrape.

He thought he could see an opening ahead and doubled his efforts. Just a few yards further and he would be in the clearing. The last few feet seemed an eternity as he clawed his way forward. The flesh on the nape of his neck crawled and all he could think about was being grabbed from behind and dragged back to his death with sanctuary so close at hand.

Click. Tap. Scrape.

His thoughts turned to Inga as he realized she would never know what had happened to him and that he would never see her again. He vowed that would not happen and redoubled his efforts.

Click. Tap. Scrape.

He burst into the clearing with such force he nearly exited the far side before he got his panicked feet under control.

Click. Tap. Scrape.

By the sound, the creature was very close. Laktos knew he wasn't out of the woods yet. He stood in a circular clearing devoid of any growth and conspicuously clean of any webbing. The clearing was eighty feet in circumference and ringed by a low stone wall. Centered and spaced evenly around the inside of the plaza were three identical stone archways fifteen feet in height and wide enough for two men to stand shoulder to shoulder in the openings.

Laktos stepped purposely towards a set of columns made of crystalline white blocks that sparkled in the filtered sunlight that entered the clearing.

He recognized this portal as the one he had used when he returned to this place from the city of dead and his fateful meeting with the wizard MOT.

He glanced to his right at another portal, and for a moment he could almost see himself with Sal as they fled through that portal and ended up on that hellish island. It seemed to him a lifetime ago, and yet it had only been less than a year.

Click. Tap. Scrape.

The sounds broke his reverie, and he quickly spoke the Ancient words that activated the portal. A low hum filled the air as the center of the archway coalesced and shimmered into focus. Laktos looked into the darkened stairwell of a long-abandoned maglev station. Cautiously, he stepped through and disappeared from the clearing. The Ancients' magical doorway closed behind him as if he'd never been.

A warning sensor interrupted Apollyon's delight. Quickly he scanned the readout. Surprise registered in his altered brain, followed by pure elation at the wonderful turn of events. "Ask for and you shall receive."

His scans had detected a power emanation from a ground source only minutes away from his current orbital position. He searched his archives until he found a signature manna field which matched the one below. "A portal doorway," he said curiously to himself. "The beginning of a new end and appropriately I shall be the keeper of the door. I shall be the new Omega!" Mentally he sent the commands which would activate his weapons systems while at the same time making a minute orbital change for the optimal firing angle. A chronometer marked the minutes until firing time.

Nervous with anticipation, he distracted himself with a diagnostic subroutine which monitored his weapons systems. He noticed the scalar particle cannon power level had dropped and now remained at eighteen percent efficiency. He backtracked the systems until he found the deficiency and tried to reroute power from alternate sources. His efforts proved rewarding, but just barely. Power was up to twenty-one percent. Not as much as he would've liked, but more than enough to punch through the atmosphere and destroy a single ground target.

While all this was happening within his multi-phased mind, a separate bank of fluidic processors tracked and plotted a second power fluctuation deep underground three-hundred, twenty-six miles due northeast from primary target. This alternative source must be the receiving portal.

The information was transferred to the scalar targeting computers and listed as a secondary target.

Apollyon fed the new data into his automatic onboard guidance system, and a course was plotted and readied for execution. He wanted to waste no time later. As soon as he destroyed the primary target, he would make for the second one as rapidly as possible. Had he still possessed hands; he would have been rubbing them together with eager anticipation. "Revenge, no sweeter fruit and I hunger."

Apollyon's inhuman patience was rewarded minutes later as he achieved primary target lock. "The beast that thou feared is me, and I shall ascend from the bottomless pit and reign from the spires of heaven!" He felt his god-like powers course through his artificial veins. Nothing could stop him from exercising his will on the world below him. He was God now.

Apollyon reached down toward the earth with his beam of scalar energy. The portal returned to standby maintenance mode, conserving its manna energy and waited for the next user to come along. Following its standard procedures, the portal plaza dispatched its cleaning servos as it had done for hundreds of years. The tiny machines bustled about the plaza, sweeping up any stray leaf or blade of grass. To the casual eye, they appeared little different from the spiders which inhabited the surrounding forest as they scurried about their business.

The surrounding forest had changed countless times over the eons, but the plaza had remained untouched by the ravages of nature and mankind. Designed to be self-repairing, it could go on as it was for a very long time, barring any unnatural catastrophe.

A piercing blue white beam of energy reached down from the sky and lightly caressed the portal plaza annihilating the stone works and the surrounding forest for a mile in radius. The air thundered as it was sucked into the vacuum left behind by the scalar beam. Hot wind whipped up a cloud of ash and debris and carried it miles away before losing its cyclonic force and scattering the remains over a wide swath of grassland.

Chapter 15

Inga sat and stared out of the window for hours, waiting. Her mind swam in lazy circles filled with eddies of thought and emotion. She felt detached from life, as though suddenly cast to sea and set adrift to find her way alone in the dark.

Yesterday they had laughed with joy about all their wonderful tomorrows—a future filled with so much promise. Now she sat alone, out of place and far from everything she had ever known. Her life had become a living nightmare. A sudden wave of homesickness made her long to be home, to be held by her mama and comforted by her papa.

She remained outwardly still as the sun slowly crept across the partly cloudy sky. Her demeanor changed slightly about midafternoon when she spotted John returning home. For a fleeting second, she thought Laktos was with him, but it was just her heart wishing it were so.

She turned her head aside at last and wept bitter tears of sorrow into his pillow. The smell of him still lingered on the soft fabric. She squeezed the pillow to her face and cried and cried until her tears ran dry. Her loss could feel no greater had they been separated by death rather than hurtful words.

Gradually, she came to understand that she really had nothing to keep her here any longer. Without Laktos, this place had no meaning for her. With a heavy sigh of resignation, she decided it was time to return to her home. For the first time since she had left, she found herself thinking that her leaving might have been a big mistake.

By the time John had reached the farm and turned Hansel out for the afternoon, Inga had reconciled herself to her fate and had nearly finished packing her few possessions.

She looked forward to seeing the plush, flower-covered slopes and the quaint tiny village near the place she'd grown up. But mostly, she just wanted to be home.

She picked up her satchel and walked into the kitchen where Sienna was preparing some pork loins for supper. Sienna took one look at Inga and knew that more bad news was yet to come. "What's this?" she asked softly.

Inga met her friend's gaze, then looked away. It was hard enough to do what she had set her heart on without seeing the hurt in Sienna's eyes. "I've decided to go back to my homeland. It's been too long since I've been away, and besides there is nothing more for me here now that Laktos has—" she choked back a sob, then with a childlike lilt she said, "I miss my mama and papa and I want to go home—that's all."

"You must follow your heart."

Inga pulled her gaze up from the floorboards and looked at Sienna. She saw the tears well up in Sienna's eyes and threw herself into her arms. They hugged each other tightly as they wept together openly.

Neither noticed the front door opening as John stepped into the house. John's happy greeting stopped about halfway out as he stepped into the house and heard the sounds of weeping coming from the cooking area. "Uh oh. This can't be good," he said under his breath as he tried unsuccessfully to head back outside.

Sienna picked her head up and between sobs said, "John. Please ready the wagon. There'll be one more trip for you to take this day."

"What on earth for?"

"No questions right now, please," she pleaded in a soft voice.

John sensed that this was not the time to argue, "Yes, my love." He gratefully headed back outside. Just outside the door he intercepted Sal, Raziel and Caruso on their way in. "Come along. You don't want to go in there right now." He grabbed the two of them by their elbows and steered them toward the barn.

The captain was not a man accustomed to being in the dark about matters. "What in Neptune's name is going on here?" he demanded somewhat gruffly.

"I'll explain what I know as I hitch the wagon."

"What kind of nightmare did we wake up to this day," Sal said quizzically. "First Prometheus, then Laktos and—and now what? Is Inga leaving as well?"

"I believe that's exactly what's about to happen," John said as he hefted the latch on the barn doors and swung them open wide.

"Oh."

"Oh. That's all?" Raziel asked, only half joking. "You never lack for something to say." He glared with narrowed eyes at his friend. "What have you done with Sal?"

Caruso interrupted their exchange. "Stow the bilge filth. This is serious."

"Yes, captain," Raziel replied, still eyeing Sal with mock skepticism.

"If it is her will to go, then we do not have the right stop her," the captain said, almost as if he were only thinking aloud rather than giving a command.

"But she—we can't let her go alone!" Sal and Raziel cried in unison.

John quietly listened to their banter as he prepared Hansel and the wagon to journey once again.

"Of course not," the captain reassured. "Therefore, I will have to go along with her."

"Not without me, you're not!" Raziel insisted. "I'm ready to get back to sea; that is, if you're willing to sail with me again, captain, considering what happened to your last ship with me at the helm."

Captain Caruso placed a paternal hand on Raziel's shoulder as he looked him dead in the eyes. "There is no other sailor finer than you. It would be my honor to have you as first mate aboard my new ship—whenever that happens." He glanced over to Sal. "And you as well."

Sal smiled in response. "That's settled, then. Who wants to tell Inga that she has company on her trip?

Speaking of which, did she happen to say where she was going?" He looked pointedly at John.

John sensed the lull in the conversation and glanced up to see everyone looking at him expectantly. "What?"

"Where did Inga say she was going?" Caruso asked.

"I actually didn't hear her say anything about leaving or where she'd go, if she'd mentioned it."

Raziel's patience was just a breath shorter than Caruso's. "Then what in blazing oceans are we doing here? And what's all this talk of leaving if such was never said?"

"Sometimes a thing doesn't have to be spoken to make it true. Believe me. I wish I were wrong about this." He finished tacking Hansel to the wagon and led him out of the barn. He was already feeling the pangs of loss for Hansel, but he had realized there was no other way. He couldn't leave Sienna and the baby here alone for the time it would take to travel to the coast and back. A journey of that distance would require several weeks. Since Inga was being as ornery as the mule, it seemed the best he could do would be to let them all take the wagon and perhaps someday, should Hansel survive, they could bring him back home. He explained his idea to the captain as they headed outside.

Inga bent over the crib and kissed Little John goodbye. She took one last look around the tiny home and realized that she would probably never see this place again. The thought pulled at her heart and threatened to start her crying all over again. She clamped down on her emotions and tried very hard not to think about this chapter of her life closing and the new one about to begin. She drew in a deep breath and picking up her bag, headed outside to give the sad news to the rest of her friends and thus begin her journey home.

Sienna followed along in silence, too stunned by the day's turn of events. She felt as if some gigantic hand had scooped up their lives and tossed them to the four corners of the earth. She felt a little scared about what might happen next and silently prayed that all of them would be taken care of by God.

The two women walked together over to the waiting men. Inga sensed that with the wagon hitched, her friends had already figured out what was going on.

Captain Caruso watched Inga and Sienna slowly approaching. Even from this distance, he could see their red-rimmed eyes and tear-streaked faces. The anguish he imagined Inga must be feeling made him feel helpless. He had developed an instant fatherly attachment to her from the first time he'd seen her looking lost and confused at the ship dock. Since then, his affection had only deepened, until one day he surprised himself by thinking of her as the daughter he'd never had. He also had made a promise to Laktos to take care of her, and he meant to keep that promise.

As Inga stepped up to the group, he suddenly had this crazy idea that he prayed would help to ease Inga's burden. In what he hoped was a jovial voice he boomed out, "Oh wonderful! You two are just in time. I've been talking with Sal and Raziel and we've decided to head back towards the coast and seek another ship."

Sal looked sideways at the captain. "We did?"

Caruso turned and gave Sal a glare that would freeze the blood in most men's veins.

Sal immediately got the unspoken message and with a firmer tone said, "Yes—yes we did."

Caruso turned back to Inga and with a gentle tone asked, "Please, Inga. Would you come with us?"

Raziel and Sal both echoed the captain's sentiments and pleaded with Inga to accompany them on their quest. The reversal of her position stunned Inga. She had been prepared to say goodbye, and now they were pleading with her to go with them. She could barely stammer out her reply. "Yes, I'll go."

"Good cheer, then!" the captain said as he hugged Inga affectionately.

Her eyes welled with tears that threatened to flow unchecked as she returned his fatherly embrace. She felt relieved of a substantial burden knowing that she would not be traveling by herself. Of course, she should've realized they wouldn't have let her go alone.

Sal could be counted on to break the moment. "And look, she's already packed—how meraviglioso." He grinned widely as he hefted Inga's bag into the wagon.

While the others went about saying their goodbyes, Sal and Raziel went into the house and gathered together all their possessions, including the captain's. Between the three of them, that didn't amount to much—mostly what they were wearing. So it only took a few minutes to pack and give Little John a silent farewell before they were back outside, ready for their long trek to the sea.

Raziel tossed his ship bag into the wagon and turned to John and Sienna. He smiled kind of crookedly as he extended his hand to John. "I don't know what to say." He hated goodbyes and felt his face redden with embarrassment.

John understood the feeling. When he stopped to think about it, he realized that the chances of his ever seeing any of these people again were slim. He thought it strange how their lives had intertwined so completely not so long ago and now. "God be with you until we meet again, friend. To all of you, Sienna and I shall never forget how you enriched our lives."

They all took turns hugging and muttering brave assurances that someday they would meet again, in spite of feeling otherwise.

John stepped back, placed his arm around Sienna's shoulder and held her close. They stood together as everyone climbed aboard the wagon and got situated.

With Caruso at his side, Sal took the reins and gave them a slight whip. Hansel perked up his ears and pulled the wagon forward, heading east. As they set off at a leisurely pace, everyone bid one last farewell.

John and Sienna watched them until they disappeared from sight. Then, with heavy hearts and feeling somewhat lonely for the company of their departing friends, they went back inside their cozy abode and gained comfort from the love they shared. John held Sienna closely. "I love you," he whispered reassuringly in her ear. "Tomorrow will be better—I promise." He had no way of knowing how wrong would be.

The sun had nearly set when Phu-Bar spotted a small dwelling in the valley below them. "Hold up!" he barked to his men. He pulled out his spyglass and studied the house. It was a simple structure made of stone and wood. A sturdy and proven design used by nearly everyone in these parts. He scanned the yard and barn, but there was nothing noteworthy, so he turned his attention back to the house. Through the window he could see no movement inside the house, but the flickering light from a lone lantern indicated someone was there.

As the sun descended behind the mountains, the fertile valley was slowly leached of color until only dull grays and muted blacks defined the terrain.

Phu-Bar lowered the spyglass and turned to his men. "I want prisoners, you malt worms! Get to it!" he ordered, pointing toward the cottage to emphasize his words. "Scotty. Stay where you are," he commanded. He didn't want any creaking sounds from the wagon alerting the occupants of the house of their impending capture—at least not until he was sure there was no way of escape.

Finnochio led the guards toward the house. They moved stealthily out ahead of Phu-Bar in a wedge formation. Phu-Bar followed at a discreet distance. Silently, they descended into the valley and passed the barn. They crept around the house until a ring of murderous men surrounded it.

Phu-Bar glared back up the road and raised his arm to signal for the wagon to be brought closer.

Sweat beads formed on Scotty's forehead as he urged the nag forward. On the seat beside him, Gropenhiney shifted nervously with every squeak and groan of the heavily loaded wagon. Secured in the back was the cannon, along with enough shot and powder to storm a fortress.

"Take it easy, up there." Frank's harried whisper drifted up from the rear.

"Shhh. Phu-Bar is nearby," Scotty said under his breath. "Do you want to get us killed? Be quiet."

Scotty pulled the wagon around until the rear was pointed at the entrance of the stone cottage at a distance of about forty feet. As silently as they could, Scotty and Gropenhiney opened up the rear tarp of the wagon and tied it off. Frank and Peat worked in the back, struggling to ready the cannon with primer and shot. If not for the seriousness of their situation, their efforts would have been comical. They were more of a hindrance to each other than help, but despite themselves, they eventually completed their task, reporting the cannon manned and ready. In their bungled haste, however, they neglected to seal one of the powder kegs—it had toppled on its side, the force of impact knocking out the plug. Opened and unnoticed on the ground, it followed the contour of the land and slowly rolled under the rear of the wagon trailing a line of black powder.

Finnochio walked over to Phu-Bar, who was waiting nearby in the darkness of some fruit trees. "The cannon is ready, sir."

Phu-Bar listened to the report in unmoving silence, his eyes hidden in deep pools of shadow. When Finnochio finished, Phu-Bar shifted his bulk irritatedly and turned his gaze to Finnochio.

Finnochio caught a glimpse of those eyes as a glint of starlight reflected from them. They seemed to say, "What are you waiting for?" and glared in the door's direction. Finnochio understood all too well what they expected of him—he just wasn't sure he had it in him. Swallowing his fear, he raised his arm, then with a swish of his wrist, he gave the signal to fire.

Sienna stirred the kettle of stew one last time before she took a taste to see if it was done. "Mmmmm, this is good. Are you ready to eat, John?"

"I was ready to eat hours ago. I'm starved, and it smells delicious." He left Little John in his cradle near the fireplace, walked into the kitchen and wrapped his arms around her waist from behind as she ladled out two servings of stew. He playfully nuzzled her neck and nibbled on the lobe of her ear. "Mmmmm, tastes good."

Giggling, she cried, "Stop it! You're going to make me spill this all over the place."

"Ohhh, nooo!" he teased.

"We'll see how funny you think lapping your food up off the floor is," she said with an impish look in her eye.

He backed off with his hands raised in surrender, "You win! You win! I'll be good."

She leaned back into him with her face slightly tilted up and turned towards him.

He leaned in and lightly kissed her offered cheek as he took his bowl of food from her outstretched hand. "Why I put up with you, I've yet to figure out," he said with a stern look in his eye. "It seems as though I must be mad—or madly in love."

"No doubt madness would be a factor," she said haughtily with a twinkle of mirth in her eye.

"Father always said that insanity was a virtue in our family—" John's reply was abruptly cut short by a piercing explosion.

"What on earth—"

A half second later the front door exploded inward, sending shards of splintered wood flying in all directions. The loud noise frightened Little John, who immediately started to wail. John could barely hear him, the ringing in his ears was so loud. He tried to reach his son, but found that his feet refused to obey his commands. He could hear Sienna screaming and his son crying as if from somewhere far away. Blood thundered in his ears and muffled all the shouting from the men now swarming into his home. Everything was happening as if in a nightmare. He looked down to see what the vague unfamiliar sensation was in his chest. To his astonishment, a large sliver of wood was protruding from his ribcage. He looked back at Sienna, "I love—"

Sienna was too horrified to do anything but watch helplessly as John fell motionless to the floor. As she attempted to reach out to help him, she was grabbed roughly by two brutish men and none too gently hustled outside.

"John!" she screamed. "John!" Her heart, her love— everything she valued gone in the wink of an eye. The shock, rapidity of it all, barely allowed her time to breathe.

Her captor slapped her hard. "Shut up, cur woman!"

It was then she heard her baby screaming. "Let me go, you pig!" She struggled to free herself. "Let me go to my baby!"

Little John's cries seemed to intensify, as if he could sense his mother's struggle to reach him. His crying became gurgled and then stopped abruptly.

She stopped her struggles and listened with all of her being for any sound from her child. Anything to put aside her horrible fear of what his silence could mean. Desperately she strained to see inside the open door, but a large man was blocking the doorway. As he stepped outside, she could see he was wiping his sword blade on one of Little John's diapers. "NOOO!" she cried hysterically.

Phu-Bar stepped forward and clubbed her on the side of the head. She was instantly knocked unconscious. "Gag her and tie her to a horse. I want her brought back to the fortress, alive."

"Yes, sir," the guard answered.

Phu-Bar was furious. If Laktos had been here, it was obvious he was long gone now. But perhaps it wasn't a total loss—the woman might still know something useful. But if not, we could use her in other ways. He turned to the remainder of his men. "Search the barn and the grounds for any clues to Laktos' whereabouts, then burn this place to the ground!"

Pointing at the guard, he barked, "Bring her!" Then climbed atop his old nag of a horse and started back toward the fortress. The guard obediently followed with his prisoner bound by the wrists and tethered across the back of his horse.

Finnochio waited until Phu-Bar was long gone before he let himself breathe a sigh of relief. All things considered; the night had gone fairly well. In fact, he felt an energy flowing through his limbs that had him wanting Scotty's attention. When this was over, he would find the time for them, but there was still work to be done. "Frank. You, Peat and Gropenhiney stow the cannon for the journey back.

Scotty and I will prepare some torches for burning this place down," Finnochio ordered.

While Scotty wrapped several sticks with oiled cloth, Finnochio set fire to a small punk pot that would be used to light the torches. With the need for stealth gone, they lit the first two torches, finished, and set them on the ground a few feet from the wagon so they could see better. When they had enough torches ready for the rest of the guards, they passed them out and set the guards to work torching the barn and garden area.

After Gropenhiney was finished with his work on the cannon, he began to spread black powder around the front of the house. When he had dumped nearly a full keg, he trailed it back to a spot near the wagon where they could light it as a fuse. His eyes shimmered a maniacal red in the flame-light of the burning barn.

John's eyes fluttered open. At first, he couldn't remember what had happened or why he was on the floor. But his memory returned with the first sensation of searing pain that swept through his body in convulsing waves. He tried to rise, but all he could manage was to lift his head only slightly. It was enough for him to see the blood that dripped from the bottom of Little John's cradle. "Oh God, nooo—" he moaned in despair. "Sienna?" he croaked out in barely a whisper, but he knew she was gone. He could feel the emptiness in his soul.

He heard a fragment of speech from outside and caught his breath. The murderous scum who had destroyed his world were still here and it filled him with a new determination. With complete disregard for his mortal wounds, he hoisted himself up off the floor. The effort nearly lost him his battle against his impending death. He held onto the wall for support as his vision turned black around the edges and tiny lights danced in his eyes.

With superhuman effort, he fought to stay alive, if only long enough to dispatch one of the butchers to hell with his own hands. Somehow, he made it to the ruined doorway and looked out into the night. He could see a group of men standing around a wagon, laughing. They were no doubt taking pleasure in their night of evil deeds. John felt a wave of nausea pass through his pierced bowels and a sense of hopelessness washed over him as he realized that he was going to die before he could take his revenge.

His tear-filled eyes stared at the ground without seeing what lay before him. Then, somewhere in the back of his mind, he recognized his one chance—but he had to act quickly. Desperate now that he had this single opportunity, he forced himself to move. With only seconds to act, his body refused to cooperate fully. With staggering uncoordinated steps, he half fell and crawled along the wall to the fireplace where he snatched the lantern from the fireplace mantle and spun for the door. His gaze passed across the cradle and for a fleeting second, he caught sight of his baby boy's dead body. His vision clouded over and threatened to leave him blind. "Please, God. Just one more second of life."

Finnochio was just about to give the order to light their makeshift fuse when movement near the house caught his eye. He turned to look and his heart jumped into his throat. Finnochio tried to shout a warning, but no air would pass his larynx. He wanted to run, but his feet remained frozen to the spot as he watched his life about to end in horrifying, nightmarish slow motion.

John's bloodied apparition filled the doorway. Behind him, a faint glow cast a surrealistic aura around his dying body. Wrapped in a yellow halo of light, he appeared as an avenging angel to Finnochio. John's last breath left his lungs and his heart stopped beating. He fell forward with the lantern still gripped tightly in his lifeless fist. The lantern globe shattered and oil sprayed out from its ruptured tank. The still burning wick quickly spread its devouring flame. It took only a second for the moving fire to flow onto the trail of black powder. The flame dashed along the length of powder toward Finnochio as if it had a will of its own.

Panic and fear prompted Finnochio to action as the fire swept across the ground towards him. He started kicking at the line of powder on the ground, trying to create a break in the fire. In his panic, he only made the situation worse. The fire which would have died away once it had reached the end of their powder line was instead scattered in all directions by his frantic half stepping. Hot embers of burning powder flew under the wagon and found more fuel to feed on. The forgotten keg ignited and sent a fountain of sparks and flames skyward. They set ablaze the loose canvas flaps of the wagon tarp. Within seconds, it turned the entire wagon into a conflagration from hell. The canvas tarp quickly weakened and the burning tatters draped down over Frank and Peat. Wrapped in a fiery shroud, they were trapped inside the inferno. Their terror-filled shrieks died behind the roar of the consuming fire.

The six other remaining guards came running at the sound of the horrific wails. They stopped just short of the wagon and stared in shock at the raging inferno. In the back of the wagon, they could see the outlines of Frank and Peat as they writhed and twisted in fiery torment inside their shroud of flames.

At that moment, all the debris that had been blown skyward fell back to the earth. A heavy deluge of sparks, burning tatters of cloth, and glowing embers rained down on the gathered men. The men instinctively raised their arms over their heads as if to ward off a heavy rain storm. The deluge was unmerciful, as if God himself was hurling the fire of the firmament down upon them for their sins of murder.

Finnochio's high-pitched wail of stark terror pierced the night like a banshee's howl as he slapped in futility at the dozens of fires burning in his hair and on his clothing. His frantic motions only fanned the flames higher.

Two guards went running off into the night—their bodies leaving a glowing trace of light as they streaked off into the field. Eventually, they stopped and fell to the earth—smoldering in the dew-wet grass, their flailing, burning bodies twitching and jerking in a macabre imitation of the living.

Finnochio saw all this and more as his life played out in slow motion before his simmering eyes. The stench of his own burning flesh filled his nostrils and caused him to wretch violently. What little fluid that remained within his broiling body burned its way up his throat and came out scalding hot. It dribbled out of his dried and cracked mouth and scorched what remained of his lower lip.

Finnochio felt none of these things, for he was burned far beyond the threshold of pain, and yet a part of him seemed to take notice of every detail as if everything were suddenly magnified a thousand times. He could see that Scotty had lain down and was quietly smoldering. Scotty looked so warm and peaceful, Finnochio decided he wanted nothing more than to just lay down bedside him and snuggle. His eyes melted away as he imagined closing them to sleep. Suddenly he felt very, very tired and he collapsed into a fiery heap next to his lover, never to awaken again.

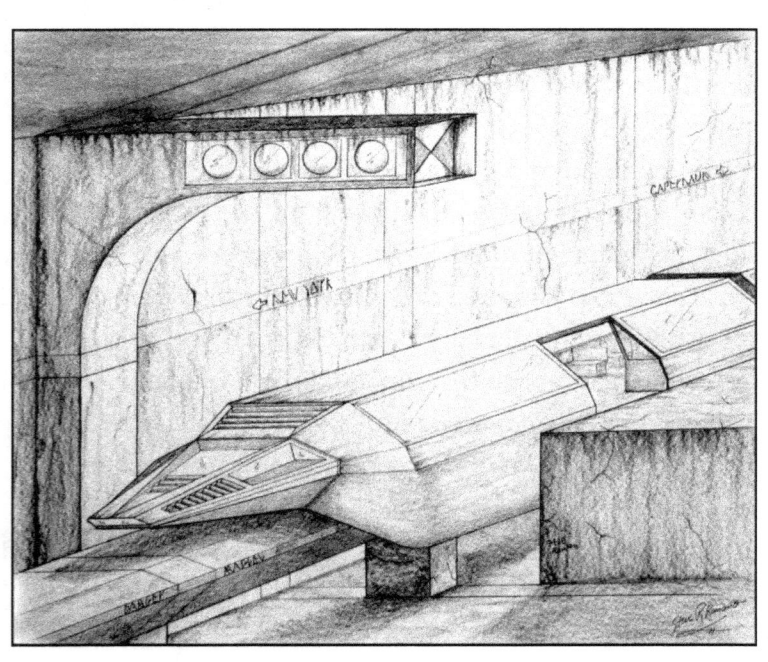

Chapter 16

Laktos stood silently, just one step away from the portal, waiting until his eyes adjusted to the nearly total blackness of the maglev station. There was no sound other than his shallow breathing. The air was musty and thick with the smell of age. As his eyes grew accustomed to the dim light that seemed to radiate from the walls, he absorbed his surroundings with a mixture of curiosity, awe and sorrow. Even after hundreds of years, the place still held the expectant air of mysterious places and far off destinations. He could almost feel the presence of the Ancients as they hustled back and forth between inexplicable locations. A soft, sorrowful sigh escaped his lips as he thought about how it all seemed so pointless now. All the wonder and magic of the Ancients had in the end become as meaningless as the lives they had engineered for themselves.

He reflected on what MOT had shown him during their last encounter, and he still found it hard to believe that the Ancients were merely mortals such as himself and not a race of gods as he had been taught to believe. The fact was, the Ancients' devices seemed perfectly suited for human use, whether or not he accepted them as mortals with supernatural powers. The skeptical part of him countered with a disturbing thought—man was created in the Ancients' image of God so it would only make sense for human beings to be able to use the Ancients' magical tools. But to what end had the old ones used their power, if this ruin was all that remained of their once mighty civilization? Were he and all the rest of humanity merely dining on the ashes of their forefathers' creation? He realized this direction of thought did nothing to lighten his somber mood, and he should be paying more attention to his surroundings—being distracted could get him killed in this sort of place.

Turning his attention outwards and abandoning that other line of thinking for a different day—lest he give himself another headache—he started down the flight of steps that would take him to the lower platform. Tattered and faded posters still clung to the dust-coated walls— advertisements for clothing, travel destinations, entertainment and a dozen other topics intended for a population that no longer existed.

Walking cautiously through scattered piles of trash layered in thick blankets of dust, Laktos didn't remember there being so much trash his last time through here. At the first landing where the stairs doubled back, he found the old remains of someone's long-abandoned refuge tucked away in a shadowed corner. A dirty mattress and several scattered cans lay amidst the detritus.

He started past without giving the place much more thought when he noticed a molded blanket covering a small mound in the center of the bed. Curious, he bent over and grabbing a corner of the old material, he gently tugged it away. The blanket disintegrated in his grasp, revealing the skeleton of a small child. Laktos studied the partially mummified remains. They were obviously that of a young girl, as evidenced by her long hair and the doll she clutched so lovingly to her skeletal breast. Her dress had deteriorated to mere threads, but Laktos could still see a trace of pink and white in the material. The mental image of her lying down alone to sleep her final slumber with her favorite toy held protectively for comfort was almost too much for him to bear.

The isolation and loneliness she must have felt were feelings he held too close to his own heart at that moment. With a force of will he didn't think he still possessed, he bit down on the aching sorrow that filled his soul; smashed and buried it beneath layers of anger.

Rage coursed through Laktos' veins. Wrath for the monsters that would cause such heartache and sorrow for the truly innocent of the world—a child. Anger for the race of the Ancients and their short-sighted folly. If this was their legacy, then he wanted no part in anything the Ancients had wrought.

"And what of God?" he thought with weary sarcasm. Truly, if he existed would he really let so much sorrow befall his children? It certainly seemed to Laktos that evil men dominated the world. His every experience since coming to this land seemed to involve the suffering of the kind and gentle-hearted people by the hands of the cruel leaders.

Laktos was really starting to hate this place. With angry strides, he continued down to the next level. The station was in darkness. He wasn't sure what to expect, but a part of him had assumed that MOT would be there waiting. But what he hadn't considered was what to do if MOT wasn't there. He paced the length of the platform as he thought about what to do.

From deep within the dark recesses of the maglev tunnel came the faint sound of air rushing forward. The sound was so faint that Laktos wasn't sure if he'd actually heard it. A second later, his doubts vanished as a stiff breeze exited the tunnel, followed moments later by the silvery fuselage of the maglev train. It whispered to a stop amidst a cloud of dust motes dimly lit by the interior lights.

Laktos stood spellbound by the wondrous machine as it floated motionless above its magnetic rail. The aura of manna energy it exuded was nearly overpowering. He had to remind himself that this device was nothing more than a contrivance built by the Ancients.

The doors on the second coach whispered open and silently beckoned him inside. He swallowed his superstitious fears and stepped over the gap and into the train. Almost immediately the doors closed, and the lights dimmed to an amber glow. The train smoothly accelerated back up the tunnel the way that it had come.

Laktos sat on the floor of the car and watched the darkness outside the windows blur past. The only actual sensation of speed was the occasional utility light that flashed by in the wink of an eye and a few open areas that he guessed were more loading platforms.

Time lost all meaning as he was hurtled along twenty stories beneath the earth. He tried not to think too much as he waited for the trip to be over, but inevitably his thoughts turned to his current situation. He wanted to be completed with this unwanted task and be on his way back to Inga as soon as possible. But his feelings on the subject were conflicted. He had to admit to himself there was a certain excitement involved with the unknown quest. Until now he hadn't realized how much he missed the adrenaline rush of discovery and the inner thrill of exploring these ancient ruins.

After everything he had endured coming this far, he hoped MOT really had something of great importance to be done so the whole effort would not have been in vain.

A vague image began to shimmer and coalesce at the front of the train car. Laktos got to his feet and stared with rapt curiosity at the ghostly apparition as it slowly solidified. He had a feeling he already knew who it would be, and a moment later wasn't disappointed. "MOT, I've been waiting for you. I came as soon as I received your summons. What's this all about?" The questions poured out of him, but before he could ask more, he was urged to silence.

MOT hushed him with a librarian's stern tone. "There's no time for questions now. Quickly grab hold of something solid and hang on for your very life!" MOT's image shimmered, then abruptly faded to almost nothing before coming into sharp focus for a split second—then he was gone.

Laktos was trying to comprehend the meaning behind MOT's warning—at least it seemed to be a warning, but he could sense nothing out of the ordinary with the train. Of course, he had only been in the thing once before so he really had no way of knowing whether something was wrong. He felt himself struggling against a slight force that tried to push him backwards. It felt as if someone was gently pushing on his shoulders and he had to push back to maintain his balance.

The utility lights in the tunnel were flashing past faster now and he realized that the train had sped up considerably. He remembered MOT's warning and quickly lay down between two seat aisles, and bracing himself against the seat backs he waited.

For what, he wondered at first. He did not know what to expect, but when it came, he knew it. It started with a muffled boom that he felt through the train's hull more than he heard it. Seconds later, a painfully loud whooshing sound roared outside the train as if all the air were being sucked out of the tunnel. Laktos felt his eardrums ache from the sudden pressure change.

The train buffeted violently from side to side. More than once, it exceeded the grip of its magnetic rail and scraped along the sides of the tunnel. The shredding steel sides screamed in tortured metallic squeals that reverberated through the train's body. To Laktos, it was a living nightmare of distorted sounds and flashes of light.

Then the lights went out. Laktos felt a sickening lightness in his bowels as the train suddenly lost all power. Safety overrides failed to operate, and the train fell more than a foot onto the now inert magnetic-rail. The impact shook the train with such force that rows of seats were sheared from their mounts and hurled towards the front of each car. Laktos was ripped from his position by a sudden jolt and felt himself pitched through the air. He heard someone scream from far away seconds before his impact with the forward bulkhead, along with several rows of seats. Stars danced in his vision for an instant in time, and then he faded into unconsciousness.

Sparks flew off the hurtling train, which was now little more than a speeding projectile careening out of control down a dark hole in the earth. The once graceful machine had been reduced to a screeching metal serpent sprouting a tail of fire as it raced headlong into the bowels of hell with Laktos trapped in its steel belly.

Minutes Earlier in Orbit

Now that Natas/Apollyon had destroyed the portal plaza, he/it followed the manna energy signature of the portal to its destination receiver and plotted a minor course correction. He could hardly believe his good fortune. It would appear his newfound purpose had been granted more than just a little guidance. Why, no sooner had he decided to take his revenge upon the globe when he had been shown two manna sources for annihilation.

He had a good feeling about this. And why not, he thought—after all "I am a god." These thoughts and many others stroked his deranged ego as his orbit brought him closer to his next target.

Minutes later, his fantasy world of destruction was interrupted by a locking tone from his targeting computer. He scanned the data spool and studied his target. The readings indicated a subterranean source. Must be an old maglev station, he thought. No matter, he would still destroy it anyway. He adjusted the aperture opening of the cannon to refocus the beam into a tighter column of energy, much the same way he had adjusted surgical lasers when he had been human.

He raised his arm/boom and extended his finger/cannon and once more felt the power surge through his mechanical body. "And power was given him over all kingdoms, and tongues and nations." A brilliant beam of blue plasma energy lanced down to the earth and obliterated his target.

His next target was the library complex where he had rediscovered himself. He set his alternate course, then waited until it was time to feed once again.

CHAPTER 17

Lendura shuffled along painstakingly. She hated being trapped in this old shell and relished the thought of soon returning to her chambers and the dark vial of Beutoxin that would transform her into her other self. "You should have used it before you came down here," the other taunted.

"Shut up!" she hissed.

She slid her hand along the wall for support as she turned a corner, then started down a steep flight of slippery stairs that led into the deeper dungeons. Water leached through the walls in dozens of places and could be heard dripping behind the stone barrier. The walls, ceiling and floor were blanketed with a thick carpet of green moss which gave everything a slippery, greasy feeling. The lighting was nearly nonexistent and the single torch that lit the stairway was on the verge of burning out.

After reaching the long hallway at the bottom of the steps, she let out a sigh of relief and rested there a moment. She glanced down the corridor to her left. The scant circle of light thrown by the torch disappeared into a well of darkness only a few feet away. The rest of the hall to the right was hidden in a veil of absolute blackness.

She had never explored down that tunnel. The few times she had started to, some distraction would arise and the idea would be forgotten for a time. Besides, she had no genuine cause or reason to go exploring. She was not an explorer by nature—no, what she desired in these stygian halls lay in the other direction, down in a part of the fortress dungeons that she knew very well.

With those thoughts in mind, she shuffled along toward her destination, passing several empty rooms on either side of the corridor until she came at last to a room on her left with a single flickering candle set upon a low, wooden table. Except for the table and a simple chair, the room was devoid of any other furnishings. She entered the room just as a low moan escaped the lips of the room's only occupant.

"Are you awake?" she croaked. She glared at his dangling form as she took the chair, turned it to face her captive and achingly sat down.

More muffled mumbling came from the pathetic creature that was once a proud man.

"Don't be shy. You were much more talkative when we first met," she crooned.

Moleinar hung limply by his wrists and ankles manacled by short chains to the wall. Although his transformation was well underway, there remained enough of his old features that Nikhole might have recognized him—but those too would fade away in another day or two, once the change was complete. Then he would be more dog-beast than man.

For now, he still had enough of his mind left to realize what was happening to him, and that knowledge terrified him to the verge of insanity. Minute by minute, he could feel his thoughts disappearing. His memories and all the experiences that made him an individual person were being devoured by the potion that poisoned his blood, but his mind refused to accept the reality of his body's senses.

"This all has to be some sort of bad dream," he thought as he tried to convince himself that he was really just sleeping off a bugger of a hangover from too much ale and a liberal dose of the mystery woman.

"Yes, it must be the woman." Even now he could hear her voice just beyond the realm of consciousness.

He tried to open his eyes, but they refused to focus. Everything had a blurry, oozing look to it as if he was viewing the world through a curtain of flowing liquid.

Strange enticing aromas tickled his olfactory. Smells that seemed repugnant one moment and delicious the next. Some were familiar, like the smell of rotting garbage, but others were brand new. He tried to put names to the odors, but it was as if he had never experienced them before.

A spasm of pain wracked his body as the potion continued to do its work. His back arched like a bow against the wall. The chains that bound him rattled against the stone as he pulled them taught in anguish.

A howling cry escaped his drawn-back and cracked lips. Blood dripped from his nose, accompanied by the sound of crushing and grinding cartilage.

His face began to distort and elongate while his brow drew back.

His screams of pure agony changed in timbre as his throat reformed around his vocal cords.

He clenched his fists so tightly that his growing claws dug deeply into his flesh. Blood pooled beneath his suspended body.

The mutation was slight, but significant. Moleinar had crossed the threshold between human being and animal. Minutes before, he had mostly resembled a man—now he mostly resembled a deformed rodent with the intelligence and disposition of a canine. His head lolled listlessly against his chest as drool ran from his mouth in long viscous beads to the floor.

Lendura watched him morphing with obvious delight. The potion was working perfectly, so far. If all went well, then by this time tomorrow Moleinar would no longer exist, and the Mole would take his place.

Satisfied that all was proceeding as planned, she painfully raised herself from the chair and exited the room. There was someone else she wanted to visit only a short distance down the corridor.

Sienna felt a burning sensation around her wrists. She tried to roll over, thinking that John must have slept on her arm again and put her hand to sleep, but she couldn't seem to move.

She lay still for a moment, temporarily baffled, caught somewhere between the twilight of the dream world and the nightmare of her reality. Ever so slowly, her mind sloughed off sleep's hazy gossamer and she came back to consciousness.

Her eyes fluttered open for a moment and she tried to make sense of her surroundings. The first thing she was aware of was that her hands were stretched up over her head, and from the coldness of the steel touching her skin, she realized they were chained to the hard surface she lay upon. About all she could move was her head—raising it enough to see that her legs were shackled as well.

It was then that her memory came back. A sob escaped from her lips as the image of her husband's dead body floated before her eyes. "Nooo!" she cried. "This can't be happening," she said to herself, but she could not deny the harsh reality of her surroundings nor the memories of what had happened.

Sienna wept uncontrollably when she was frightened by a sudden terrible scream so filled with horror and suffering, it made the hairs across the tops of her arms stand up. Her breath got caught in her throat, then panic gripped her heart with fear of her unknown fate—would she be tortured unmercifully like the poor soul whose screams rent the air? She tried hard not to imagine what horrific deed could cause such torment, but the screaming only fueled her imagination with terror. She had never been so scared in all her life, not even on the day Laktos saved her family from certain death.

Frantic with fright, she pulled and wrestled with her shackles until her wrists and ankles were sore and bloody.

Exhausted and feeling an overwhelming sense of hopelessness without John and her baby, she gave up and just prayed for a quick death.

Sienna woke up from a half sleep that she hadn't even realized she'd slipped into. She did not know how long she had been out, but she was relieved the screaming had stopped. It was then she sensed another's presence in the room standing next to her at the head of the rack, but Sienna could not turn her head far enough to see who or what it was. "Please, whoever you are. Please help me," Sienna pleaded.

A coarse chuckle was the only reply to her pleading, followed by the sounds of shuffling feet as an old woman inched her way into view and stood over Sienna. The woman's cataract gaze traveled the length of Sienna's body, making it shiver involuntarily with fear.

"Who are you?" she asked. "Let me loose, please. My child, he needs—"

Lendura's voice cackled with delight. "Your child is dead as you shall soon be."

Sienna did not try to hide her grief. "Why? Why have you done this? I don't even know who you are."

"It's not who I am that's important—it's who you know."

"What?" Sienna's confusion seemed to amuse the wretched woman.

Lendura cackled as she gently patted Sienna on the cheek in a matronly manner. "There, there, child. Don't worry. It'll all be over soon—then you can rest."

Sienna was repulsed by the evil woman's touch and turned her cheek away as best she could. "Don't touch me, you filthy hag!"

Lendura made a tisk, tisk noise of disapproval. "Not very nice."

She stepped out of Sienna's sight for a moment, then Sienna felt something cold on her inner arm followed by the sharp prick of a needle.

"That should help improve your attitude," Lendura crooned.

"What have you done?" she demanded, already knowing the answer—she could feel the effects of something foreign in her system. The powerful potion was already making her vision swim and her head feel light. "Pleash don—" she managed to slur before her eyes closed.

Lendura leaned in very close to Sienna's face. "Now tell me about Laktos. I want to know everything."

236

Chapter 18

Inga sat quietly, staring back at the road. She hadn't spoken since shortly after their departure from the farm. And even though she could hear the others quietly talking, she paid them little mind, for her thoughts were far from them. She couldn't stop thinking about Laktos. She worried about where he was—if he was all right. But these thoughts did nothing to comfort her, and worse, they caused her to doubt her decision to leave and return to her home across the ocean. So eventually she had just stopped thinking about anything and just stared emptily at the scenery as it passed slowly by.

Raziel dozed comfortably, stretched out next to her. Behind her, she could hear Sal and Caruso discussing their route to the coast. Sal drove the wagon, while Caruso studied a crude map drawn out by John. "It says here that we travel along this swamp for nearly a day before the road turns northeast. According to John, that was as far as he had explored this part of the country."

"Where do we go from there?" Sal asked.

"We cross an old bridge that leads to the north. Once across, we'll turn directly east until we reach the ocean. From there, we just head north again until we reach the village of Bost."

"Merda. Why do I have the feeling it just can't be that easy? Non dimentichero mai questo viaggio."

"What?" Caruso gave Sal a questioning look.

"Never mind," Sal answered distractedly. "You know. Something about this part of the road looks familiar to me."

"Do you think you've been here before?" the captain asked.

Suddenly, Sal had a moment of clarity which triggered his memory. "This is where John found us! Hey, Raziel. Wake up!"

Raziel opened his eyes. "What?" He sat up and shook off his sleepy state. "What do ya want? Are we there yet?" he said, sounding grumpy.

Sal reined in Hansel and brought the wagon to a stop. "Don't you recognize this place? This is where John pulled us from the swamp."

"I think you're right," Raziel agreed. He climbed out of the wagon and hopped to the ground next to Sal. Together the two men, followed by a very curious Inga, walked over to the embankment where they had dragged Inga's unconscious body ashore. It seemed like only yesterday that they had heard John call to them from this very spot, beckoning them to safety.

Inga could still see deep grooves in the muddy bank as evidence of their struggle to escape the mire. She looked out over the swampy landscape and saw the horrible conditions that Sal and Raziel had endured to save her life. She became overwhelmed with emotion and tears started to flow down her cheeks. The events of the day had drained all of her emotional reserves, and yet being here and seeing for herself the hardship and suffering these two men had endured on her behalf filled her with a brotherly love that swelled her heart to its bursting point.

Sal and Raziel both turned at the sound of her soft sobbing to see her crying unashamedly. Immediately, they both stammered, comically tripping over their tongues and babbling apologies for bringing her to this horrid place.

Inga could not help but laugh at their boyish awkwardness and threw her arms around them both, squeezing them tightly. "Thank you," she said.

The three of them stayed that way until a rather gruff throat-clearing caught their attention. Still huddled together, they all turned to see Caruso standing with his hands on his hips, glaring at them with a bemused glint in his fatherly eyes.

"This is where we—" Raziel sputtered, feeling like a child caught with his hand in the cookie jar.

"I gathered that," the Captain said. "But if you're all through reminiscing, I don't relish the idea of camping here tonight. As I recall, part of your tale involved a rather gigantic serpent."

Sal had a sudden urge to look over his shoulder. How could he have forgotten about the snake that had tried to eat him? "It's time to go, adesso, right now."

The three immediately separated. With nervous backward glances, they and Caruso climbed back aboard the wagon and set off down the road.

A few tranquil hours later they came to a shallow gorge spanned by a log and timber bridge. "This must be the bridge that John told us about," Caruso said. "Once we cross this, we'll be in unexplored territory."

"It doesn't look very sturdy," Inga whispered under her breath, afraid to voice her concerns too loudly for fear of jinxing them.

Sal gave her what he hoped was a reassuring wink as he gave Hansel a slap with the reins that started them across the rickety span.

Hansel stopped just at the edge of the bridge and looked out across the slightly twisted roadway to the far side.

"Come on, boy," Sal urged gently.

Hansel gazed back over his shoulder at Sal as if to say, "Are you crazy?" Then he took a tentative step forward, then another, and another, until finally the wagon was on the structure.

The bridge creaked and moaned in protest, but otherwise the crossing was uneventful, and the small group released a collective sigh of relief when they finally pulled to a stop on solid ground again.

Hansel made his feelings plain by raising his tail and lightening his personal load by several pounds.

"Let's camp here for the night," Caruso suggested. "I'm worn out."

"That's a good idea," Sal echoed. "It looks like we have just enough time to set up in the little daylight we have left."

Working together, it didn't take long for them to get their home for the night prepared and a nice cozy fire going to ward off the night.

They set Hansel out to graze while the others sat around the fire and made idle speculation about the journey ahead of them.

As the hour grew late, Inga found herself nodding off as she stared mindlessly into the fire. She had wrapped herself in a blanket an hour earlier and had sat apart from the others to be alone with her thoughts. The fire danced before her sleepy eyes as her mind replayed the events of the day.

She missed Laktos, but through willpower alone she pushed him as far from her thoughts as possible, which wasn't far enough. Tonight, she realized would be the first night that she would sleep without him beside her. Her heart balled up into a knot in her chest and something very much like panic kept her from breathing for a second. She swallowed hard and pushed that sickening lump down deep where she couldn't feel it anymore and lay herself down next to the fire. She stared into the flames for a long time before her eyes finally succumbed to strain and she fell into a troubled sleep.

Inga Dreamed

She ran laughing across a sunny, flower-adorned hillside until she reached the top where she threw herself down, tumbling end over end all the way to the bottom. Before she could lift herself from the ground, Lucky was there, sloppily licking her face.

She flung her arms around his scruffy neck and gave him a big hug. Now it was Lucky's turn to squirm and try to get away from her affections. The two of them play wrestled in the tall grass for a few minutes. Then without warning, Lucky jumped back and started barking at her.

She sat back with a big silly grin on her face and wondered just what game he was playing now.

They always played games together on her way home from school, where he would wait outside the gate for her every day. Today they were playing tag-me, or at least they had been. Now she was sitting in the tall grass trying to figure out Lucky's new game.

Suddenly he took off up the hill and in seconds he was gone, his barks fading quickly into the distance.

She picked herself up and brushed some grass from her pleated yellow skirt. After picking up her school books, she started up the hill after him.

She stood next to a great oak tree, which spread its noble limbs out to catch the sunshine. But there was no longer any sun to catch on this day, and the dark clouds and rain seemed somehow appropriate for the occasion. It certainly underscored her mood.

Her father finished patting the earth down with his shovel, and she could tell by the shuddering of his shoulders that he was silently weeping beside the tiny grave. She had never seen her papa cry before. He was always so unflappable about life's minor tragedies that his tears for Lucky tore at her heart almost as much as losing Lucky himself.

She turned her head into her mother's apron and let her grief flow into the comforting embrace of her mama.

The following morning dawned bright and cheery with the fresh smell of dew evaporating in the spring air. The earth had cladded itself in multitudes of vibrant colors, in many variations from pastel-colored flowers to brilliant shades of the large-winged butterflies sipping on nectar. Lazy white clouds floated carefree in the pristine blue sky, accompanied by flocks of birds returning to their summer region.

Inga awoke lying on her back staring up at the deep blue sky. It was promising to be a gorgeous day, but she hardly noticed. Her sleep had been fretful and not at all replenishing. Despite the cheerfully sunny day, her mood remained somber and withdrawn with the remnants of her dream still haunting her. She was filled with a sense of loss and was yearning to be home as soon as possible.

She put her hands in the small of her aching back and tried to stretch out some of the kinks.

Sal stepped around from the other side of the wagon where he and Caruso had been engaged in quiet conversation, and smiled at Inga. "Buon giorno, Inga. Did you sleep well?"

"Except for the rock that poked me in the ribs all night, I guess that I slept well enough. And you?" Inga tried hard to sound upbeat, but inside her head, her words felt hollow.

"Buona. I mean yes, I slept. Are you hungry?" Sal stumbled along with his conversation studiously trying to ignore Inga's false joviality. "I found some wild onions and potatoes, and the captain snared a rabbit. We made some soup, which should be just about done." Sal grabbed a pot off the side of the wagon and filled it from a kettle slung over glowing coals on John's makeshift stand. "Mmm. Bene, bene." He handed the bowl to her. "Come on, mangiare."

She didn't feel hungry, but took the bowl from him and sat down to eat, if only to avoid any protests. Her feelings changed as the aroma of freshly cooked food wafted toward her. The stew smelled delicious and soon had her stomach growling in anticipation. She took a first taste and from that point on she didn't stop until the bowl was empty.

Finished, she looked up from her meal, slightly embarrassed after realizing she had ignored everything around her as she ate. She half expected everyone to be staring at her, but they all seemed to be busy making preparations for departure. Relieved, she went about washing her pot and helping to repack their supplies.

Conversation between them all was light and mostly oriented toward their tasks. It wasn't long before all was in order and ready to go.

The captain was the last to board the wagon. Sal gave Hansel a quick whistle, and he started up the road. "What's our heading, captain?"

"We follow this road east to the shoreline and then north to Bost. If we're lucky, we should be there in about a week."

"Well, let's pray for some luck then," Raziel said gloomily.

Chapter 19

Laktos first sensory input was excruciating pain. It pulled him from the depths of unconsciousness and left him painfully aware of the real world he still inhabited. When he opened his eyes, he saw only uninterrupted darkness. He fought back a momentary feeling of panic that he might have been blinded in the crash. Closing his eyes helped ease the fear. If he was going to survive, he would have to deal with one thing at a time. His first priority was to get himself free from this wreck and out of this subterranean nightmare.

Laktos felt pressure around his body and realized that he was pinned under a pile of debris. He lay still for a moment and tried to assess his injuries. He could feel his fingers and toes wiggle—that was a good sign his foolish neck wasn't broken, but when he tried to shift his weight around, he was rewarded with a knife-sharp pain that ran the length of his left leg from his knee to his ankle. He tried to probe the wound with his fingers, but he was pinned too tightly.

His arms were pressed across his chest as if a giant hand were crushing him. No matter how hard he tried, he couldn't manage more than a few agonizing inches of movement in any direction.

He could feel the icy hand of terror grip his heart as he mentally saw himself trapped in this dark, claustrophobic place with no hope of getting any help; entombed all alone in the blackness, waiting for the end to come. He wondered whether his friends and in particular Inga would ever know where he was and what became of him.

Would Inga even care if she knew? He wished he could take it all back. He wished that he had never decided to help MOT. In his imagination, he saw himself still at the farm with Inga and their friends. Their lives unchanged and unchanging as the years faded past, and they all grew old together. He wrapped himself in this fantasy world, and without realizing it, he slipped into a troubled slumber.

In Laktos' Dreams

Laktos turned to face Raziel and Sal, who stood with their backs to the stern rail. He absently gazed past them and marveled at the magnificence of the vast sea. The ocean spread out behind the ship until the curvature of the earth stole it from view. He felt the sea breeze against his face and the smell of the saltwater in the crisp, cool air. The wind snapped the rigging, making bell-like tones that melded with the creaks and groans of the ship to create a symphony of music for his ears. For that brief moment, he felt that all was right with the world.

The sunlight captivated him as it sparkled on the wave tops. He wasn't sure at first glance, but there seemed to be something odd about the color of the water.

Abruptly, a brilliant beam of blue light touched down from the heavens and struck the ocean many leagues behind them.

Laktos was instantly on his feet. "Look!" he shouted, pointing past his friends in its direction.

Sal and Raziel turned and stared in astonishment at the awesome spectacle. "Merda!" Sal shouted in frightened disbelief.

Raziel stood with his mouth agape. "Mother of god!" he whispered in near silence, stunned by what he was witnessing.

Clouds coalesced on the surface of the water where the beam touched down. A towering column of super-heated steam shot skyward. Thousands of feet high, it condensed where it met with the cool air above. Rain clouds formed almost instantly. Thunder, so loud it pained their ears, rolled across the heavens. The wind howled like a banshee from Hades. It whipped the Morning Star from every direction at once. The sky turned black and ominous. Thick clouds of vaporized sea water blocked out the sun and turned the blissful day into a terrible nightmare.

The ship was rocked from stem to stern by the rising swells. Heavy rain poured down in dense sheets that pounded on the deck of the beleaguered ship.

The hammering rain snapped Raziel out of his stupor and he barked out commands. "Laktos! Secure the forward hatch!" He had to shout to be heard over the gale-force winds. "Sal! Hurry! Get the captain!"

Raziel gripped the wheel with sure hands and put his entire being into his fight against the power of the sea.

Laktos felt himself choking on a mixture of sea and rainwater with each labored attempt to breathe. He had succeeded in reaching the main mast and was grasping for a loose stay line when he heard Sal yelling.

"Look!" Sal cried.

Laktos strained to see through the downpour to where Sal was pointing. "Oh, my god!" he uttered.

A wall of water roughly fifty-feet high was rapidly bearing down on them. All that he could do was hold on and watch helplessly as the killer wave swept towards them at unbelievable speed. The thunderous roar of the wave surrounded him and he was instantly engulfed in the liquid nightmare.

His Dream Morphed to Another Place and Time

His head broke the surface in a froth of bubbles. He gasped for air as he tried desperately to swim to shore, but the rushing waters refused to yield. He screamed a plea for help, but disturbingly, his friend just stood there on the river bank not moving an inch.

It took all his effort to keep his head above the swirling water as he went round and round, each time faster than the last as he neared the center of the powerful vortex. With all his strength, he made one last effort to break away from the roaring maw. "Help me!"

But his long-time companion made no effort to save him. Instead, he looked on impassively, waiting for the inevitable.

The presider made eye contact with his old friend and in that fragment of time, a single thought passed between the gulf that separated them— "Why?" Then the awful weight of his friend's betrayal dragged him under the rushing waters. Exhausted and soul-sick, he did not try to regain the surface. His warm tears mixed with the cool water that engulfed him. He gazed up and watched the pattern of light reflecting on the surface fade from sight as he sank deeper into the black unknown. His listless body jerked spasmodically as his lungs filled with water.

Laktos awoke in a panic, feeling the weight of all that water pushing down on him. It took him a moment to remember where he was and that the weight was not water but all the wreckage piled on top of him.

Desperately he squirmed and wriggled beneath the pile of broken seats, but he only aggravated his injuries and caused himself a lot of pain.

Panting from the effort, he lay still and tried to think of a way out of his dire situation. He speculated whether MOT could help in some way, but the old wizard was only a spectral image, and Laktos could see no way he could help—at least not on this side of life.

Clink

Laktos was immediately alert to the sound and strained to hear anything more. Was it just his imagination, or was he no longer alone? That thought should have brought him some modicum of comfort, and it might have if it hadn't dawned on him that the only thing that could be down here was probably looking for food. Now he had something worse to imagine.

Now he could hear a scratching sound, as if whatever was out there had sensed his presence and was furiously digging through the rubble to reach its next meal.

He felt more movement up near his head and suddenly realized there was more than one unwanted guest for dinner. This was not good and getting worse by the second. With supreme effort he twisted and pushed outwards in any direction, simply trying to make any room at all from which he could get some leverage. He ignored the pain it brought and strained his muscles to the snapping point.

Abruptly, the pile shifted and part of the wreckage fell away, freeing his right arm and part of his upper torso and head. "Thank the Ancients!" he blurted out.

With his head exposed, he found that all was not in total darkness as before. A very faint light filtered in from some unknown source and turned the blackness into shifting patterns of grey. Being able to see even a little helped raise his spirits, and for the first time he felt that there might be hope for him after all. That was when he heard the unmistakable sound of a dog panting. He stared into the grayness looking for the animal, but all he could see was a black shadow moving carefully through the rubble getting closer with each labored breath.

He squirmed more, but it seemed the debris had shifted all that it could without the help of some outside force. "Damn," he said with resignation.

He laid his head back and nearly jumped out of his skin when he looked straight into the face of a small creature. The cat calmly gazed back at him, unfazed by his startled reaction. Laktos quickly realized that he was looking at a Siamese cat. The feline had a cream-colored body that turned to a deep chocolate brown on his legs, head and tail. His chin, chest and belly as well as the tips of his paws were white and Laktos could see that the pads underneath were pink.

The cat stared back at him with piercing blue eyes for a minute, then apparently bored with what he saw, groomed himself fastidiously.

Laktos laughed. He didn't know why, but suddenly everything seemed hilarious. Maybe it was his relief at being partially freed from the weight of the wreckage, or that his nightmare of becoming a food source appeared remote for the moment. It might have been his body simply coming down from an adrenaline high, but regardless of the cause, the more he thought about how absurdly ironic his predicament was, the harder he laughed. "Oh, God. You have one hell of a sense of humor to bring me to this."

As irrational as it might have seemed, it felt good to release some of his built up apprehension. He turned his attention back to the cat. "Well, who are you, my little friend? Did you come to save me or eat me?"

The cat meowed loudly as if in response to his questions, then went about licking its foreleg as if he no longer had any interest in Laktos.

Laktos slowly raised his arm toward the cat, not wanting to frighten it away. He was actually very grateful for the companionship and wanted to touch the cat just to be sure it was real and not just the figment of a damaged mind.

The cat stopped grooming himself and watched Laktos with curious blue eyes.

Laktos looked into those eyes and thought he beheld a glint of intelligence along with something else—mirth? "Maybe I am insane—or dead," he muttered to himself.

The cat purred loudly as if in answer and hopped down closer to his side and stretched his head up to meet Laktos' reaching hand. He pushed hard against Laktos, luxuriating in the caress of a human.

Laktos scratched behind the cat's ear, which only made the cat purr louder and push harder against his fingers.

"Good."

Laktos was jolted as if lightning had struck him. He jerked his hand back and stared at the cat. "Did I—did you just speak to me?"

The cat was undoubtably looking directly at Laktos. And by the sounds of its purring, it seemed as if the cat was trying to talk with him.

Laktos' experience with Prometheus gave him a curious thought. "I wonder." He tried to quiet his mind as he had learned to do when talking with Prometheus, then reaching out he gently touched the cat. Immediately, he sensed the cat's thoughts. "Hello," Laktos said in his mind.

"Lo," he replied. "Rub." The cat purred and once more pushed itself against Laktos' hand.

"OK, OK. You're an insistent little bugger. Do you have a name?"

"Doodles."

"What kind of name is that for a cat?" he said as his eyes caught a flicker of light near his feet. "How about if I just call you Dood?" he asked.

The cat purred as if to say "Yes" while pushing against Laktos' hand.

The dog meanwhile had picked her way through the wreckage and now sat at his feet watching their exchange. She must have been jet black because all Laktos could see of her was the soft shine in her big brown eyes and a vague silhouette against the darkness.

"Is the dog with you?" he asked.

"Days."

"Days?" Laktos guessed from the reply that Dood and the dog had been together for a while now, but it wasn't clear how long that had been. Of course, how long mattered little, for it was obvious that the two were looking out for each other and had developed a strange kind of friendship.

"Does the dog have a name?"

"Dog-grrrs."

"Doggers?"

Dood purred and rubbed his cheek against Laktos' idle fingers.

Still watching the dog, Laktos said, "Doggers. Come closer."

Her ears picked up at the sound of her name and Laktos could hear the swish of her tail wagging, but he could detect no other motion.

Dood meowed loudly as if echoing Laktos' request.

Doggers got up and her tail immediately started wagging briskly behind her. She picked her way through a row of upturned seats and cautiously approached to a point barely within Laktos' reach and waited.

Laktos stretched out his hand until he felt the side of her head. Her fur felt soft under his fingertips as he gently pet her. "Can you hear me, too?"

She did not answer in his mind like Prometheus or Dood, but she unmistakably nodded her head to reply yes.

Although he did not hear any actual words, he could sense a powerful feeling of empathy coming from Doggers, as if she could speak to him through emotions rather than words. From her, he felt intense feelings of sympathy for his pain and a desire to help.

An image of a dog formed in his mind—presumably Doggers—her leg stuck in some sort of trap. Hurt and terrified, she was ready to gnaw off her paw to set herself free, when a kindly human and his cat rescued her and nurtured her back to health. That man died months ago at the hands of marauders. She and Dood were almost killed themselves trying to protect their human friend. Ever since that day, the two had been wandering aimlessly across the countryside, following in the direction of their noses.

Laktos' aching leg reminded him of his dire situation. "Maybe I should just chew my leg off, eh Doggers?"

Doggers immediately moved just out of his view somewhere near his feet and started pulling and tugging on what felt like his leg. He had a momentary fear that she had taken him literally. "No! No! I wasn't serious!" he struggled against the rubble which was pinning him down and found that he now had gained some freedom of movement in his legs.

He now understood what Doggers was doing—pulling some debris away from his feet. "Come on, Doggers—you can do it!" he encouraged.

Doggers was putting her heart into it as she growled deeply and whipped her head from side to side, pulling with all her might. At the same time, Laktos wriggled and pushed at the pile with his free arm, and although he was still pinned, he could feel they were making progress. "Keep pulling, Doggers!"

Dood purred nonchalantly and went about licking his forepaws as if completely engrossed with his personal grooming and blissfully unaware of the drama playing out before him. The silent swishing of his tail was the only outward sign of his apprehension.

Suddenly, the pile shifted and Laktos felt a great weight slide off of his side. Now that both his arms were unrestrained, he was able to help Doggers push the rest of the rubble off his legs, and minutes later, he was free.

He crawled shakily to his feet and took a deep breath of air as he stretched—it felt fantastic to be able to move and flex after being constricted for so long.

As soon as he worked out a few of the kinks in his muscles, he turned his attention to his rescuers. Bending down on one knee, he reached out to Doggers. She came over to him and sat down, raising her right paw out to Laktos. There was no mistaking this gesture as Laktos took her paw in his hand and shook it. "Thank you. I owe you my life, my friend."

Doggers' moist eyes glinted as a silly looking grin formed around her long, drooping tongue. Her happily wagging tail quickly swept a clean wide arc in the dust behind her.

Laktos could feel Doggers' joy at having helped free him and also her eagerness to stay with him. It was easy for him to see what he had to do. "How would you two like to join me on my quest?"

Doggers stood up on her hind legs and gave an enthusiastic bark as she pawed the air.

Dood was more reserved in his response. He simply meowed, then led the way out of the wreckage. His tail stood straight up like a sign post as he headed back the way he and Doggers had come into the train wreck.

Doggers would not be outdone by a mere cat, so she tore out ahead of him, practically trampling Dood in her haste to be the one in the lead.

Laktos did his best to keep up. He squeezed his way through a fracture in the trains' side and slid down the hull to the ground. The drop sent a wave of agony up his left leg and he collapsed to the ground with a groan.

It seemed as though only a second had elapsed before Doggers was suddenly there, licking his face and silently urging him to get up with a quiet whine.

Laktos staggered back to his feet and once again started on his way. The tunnel was not completely dark and he could see by the faint light just enough details to pick his way safely through the train wreckage.

The damage was so extensive that he could hardly recognize the torn and shredded steel as the once streamlined machine he had been aboard. It was a miracle that he had survived the crash and another that he had been befriended by benevolent creatures. "Maybe there is a God," he mused.

He spent the next hour following Dood and Doggers through a labyrinth of twisted metal, broken glass, and shattered plastics until finally they were past the worst of the wreckage.

The tunnel stretched out before him until it faded into darkness in the far distance. To him, it looked as though it went on forever—or until it reached the gates of hell.

He was glad for the company of his new friends. Doggers pressed herself against his right leg, and he let his hand rest gently upon her head. Laktos idly scratched behind Doggers' ear as he gave some thought to what he should do next. He felt he should still press on and try to reach MOT. Whatever danger MOT was in probably had something to do with the train wreck. Once again, he gazed down that long, dark tunnel. He realized he had little choice.

MOT was somewhere down at the end of that tunnel, and if he hoped to find him, that was where he would have to go.

"Come on, Doggers. Dood. It's time to go see a wizard."

The three of them set off down the long tunnel, heading toward an uncertain future.

Epilogue

Prometheus soared through the sky with barely any effort, gliding along on thermal updrafts. His sharp eyes scanned the earth beneath for any sign of his quest. So far, his search had proven to be fruitless, but he was not ready to give up hope yet. He had seen no living person since he had left the farm and his human friends.

The earth beneath him had grown colder and more barren the farther north he had flown. For the last day or so, he had seen no signs of life at all—flora or fauna. The landscape beneath him was a bleak terrain of monotone white with only occasional rock outcroppings breaking the monotony—it was as if he were the only living being on a frozen planet.

The idea of being alone did not bother him, for dragons were usually solitary creatures. But he yearned to find the legendary cave of the ice dragons. He felt driven by some inner compulsion that would not let him rest until he'd exhausted himself searching to find out whether the myths were true.

He banked slightly to his left and felt the wind currents support his wings like invisible hands.

If only the myths were true—he tried to imagine what it would be like to live among his own kind again. Vague familiar memories tugged at the dark corners of his mind as if—His eyes locked on a dark speck moving slowly across the ice. "A human?!" He started a gradual descent that would carry him over the figure far below. His mind burst forth with a thousand questions to which he had none of the answers.

He scanned the horizon in all directions for some clue to what this human was doing way out here in the middle of nowhere, but there was nothing for as far as he could see.

How was it possible that the man had traveled this far into the wastelands without supplies of any kind? It seemed impossible, yet here he was.

Prometheus rapidly descended and quickly closed the distance. The human seemed oblivious to his silent approach as he entered a narrow canyon and disappeared from view.

Prometheus landed just outside the entrance. The frozen ground made a soft crunching noise beneath his talons.

Ahead of him was a very narrow cleft that rose straight up for several hundred feet in between two sheer walls of ice. He shifted nervously from claw to claw as he weighed the risks of following the human into this crevasse.

A dragon was most vulnerable on the ground, and the tight confines of the crevasse would hamper his movements further. Flight would be impossible if he did not have the room to open his wings. And yet in spite of his forebodings he found himself walking forward in the footsteps of the man.

The ice canyon wound its way deeper into the glacier in a serpentine fashion. Prometheus cautiously followed the human's footsteps through a maze of twists and turns that were both confusing and familiar at the same time.

His claws walked unfaltering as if they had traveled this path before, and yet he could find no memory of this place and was certain he had never been here before—or had he?

He rounded another bend and stopped in his tracks. His heart skipped a beat as he tried to digest what was before him. He could hardly believe what he was seeing. The fissure had opened out into a small bowl-shaped canyon, the sides of which appeared as a waterfall frozen in mid flow.

Directly ahead of him was a fissure in the glacier's face that rose fifty feet overhead. To either side of the opening stood the carved likeness of two immense dragons poised as sentinels ready to strike anyone who dared pass them.

Between the silent guardians stood the human he had followed, wrapped in several layers of dingy animal furs. He was looking at Prometheus with a lopsided grin and a bemused twinkle in his bloodshot eyes. "I knew you'd return to us someday."

Prometheus was too stunned to do more than utter his surprise as recognition of the man slowly dawned on him. "You!"